I0592553

First published by JMH World Publishing in 2018
This edition published in 2018 by JMH World Publishing
Copyright © JM Hart 2018
jmhartwriter.com
The moral right of the author has been asserted.
The Emerald Tablet: Convergence
EPUB: 9781925786187
Cover design by Juan Padron
Publishing services provided by Critical Mass

CONVERGENCE

BOOK THREE OF THE EMERALD TABLET SERIAL

JM HART

JHM WORLD PUBLISHING

ABOUT CONVERGENCE: BOOK THREE IN THE EMERALD TABLET SERIAL

As doomsday approaches, can the teens accept their destiny in time to protect their world?

Seven special teens. A deadly ancient evil. Can they combine their unique powers and halt the infection before humanity is obliterated?Shaun is dying. The plane's engine is failing. Kevin must open a portal to catch the falling plane and save Shaun's life. Sophia is terrified of God's plan for her. Plagued by visions of planetary devastation, she prays Shaun and Kevin can reach her in time to save humanity.

Click the link and buy book three, **Convergence** in the Emerald Tablet action-packed supernatural dystopian urban fantasy series filled with daring teens, page-turning adventures, and otherworldly powers.

I dedicate this book to my daughter Bianca – never stop dreaming.

For as by a man came death, by a man has come the resurrection of the dead.

1 Corinthians 15:21-22

INTRUSION: KEVIN. AUSTRALIA

"Why have you got a backpack on, K?" Alex asked, hanging upside down on the sofa.

"We're hiking up to the lookout," Kevin said, adjusting the straps.

"Can I come, pleeeassse, can I come?"

They were gathered in the front room that overlooked the driveway, waiting for Daniel. The room was filled with light and the house smelled of sage and lemongrass. Kevin missed his nanna. Even though he felt her presence, she was always just out of sight. With his backpack ready and strands of his hair caught in the corner of his mouth, he said, "No. You can't come."

Daniel walked into the room. "Get your hair out of your mouth. You will be coughing up fur balls like a cat." Shaun and Tim laughed at the same time and they both cleared their throats.

"Dad, can I come? *Pleeeease*?" Alex stretched his neck as far back as he could looking up at Daniel. "*Please, please.*"

"No, buddy, it's just the big boys this time. Maybe you can come next time."

"But she's going and she's not a boy. Why does she get to go?"

"That's enough, Alex. We need a man to stay back and look after the girls."

Jade huffed and put her hands on her hips.

"What?" Daniel said, looking at her pose.

"That was two sexist comments in a row."

"Alex, you are getting me into trouble here, buddy," Daniel said.

Jade stepped towards Alex and put her hand on his shoulder, crouching down to his height. "You can't come because we have long legs and you would have to run to catch up with us and that would make you very tired. Then you would have a miserable time and want someone to pick you up. Do you understand?" Jade said.

"Yep, you don't want me to come because I am small," he said, stomping away.

"Don't you think that was a bit harsh?" Daniel asked.

"No, he now knows the truth. It's just logistics; there is nothing emotional about the decision."

Shaun, Tim and Daniel headed out the door with Jade and Kevin bringing up the rear.

They started heading for the green paddock where a couple of cows were grazing. They all jumped over the white fence, ignoring the cows.

"Hold up," Daniel said. "Shaun, take off your pack. Kevin, I want you to carry it."

With a smirk on his face, Shaun dropped a strap off one shoulder and then the other, and handed the pack to Kevin.

"What? *Daaad*, what gives?" Kevin said, taking the straps.

"Take yours off and give it to Shaun to carry."

The smile fell from Shaun's face. Together they all walked in silence until a brush turkey ran in front of them. It did a random dance and then took off into the bushes.

"Why do you always have your hand in your pocket?" Tim asked Shaun. "You playing with yourself?"

"You're disgusting! It's none of your business."

"That's rich, coming from you," Tim said.

Kevin and Jade had a bird's-eye view walking behind them. His dad looked at Shaun as if waiting for an answer too. He handed Tim the binoculars to carry. Shaun was ignoring Tim, but he pulled his hand out of his pocket, adjusted the straps on Kevin's backpack and kept walking. Kevin could feel his dad's tension, Tim's excitement and the sadness in Shaun, plus the cogs in Jade's head were spinning faster than the rest of them put together.

"What are you thinking?" he asked. "You really want to know?"

"Sure."

"About S = k log W. Entropy, it's a mathematical formula for a concept measuring from order to disorder and it can't be reversed because of the arrow of time, which is the direction of events that always moves forward. Like an apple fallen from a tree can never levitate itself back onto the tree, but we could make apple pie. If we take broken colored bottles and, for instance, glued them together they will never be the same, but the fragments can be turned into a stained-glass window creating a beautiful new state of order — perhaps ... to create order from disorder lies within our thoughts. Order is there but our perception only sees the disorder until we create a sense of order. But we can't go back to the original state." *Why not, why can't we go back in time or forward for that matter?* Jade stopped talking, aware she was lost in her own train of thought. She looked at Kevin and smiled, wondering what he thought of her mental rambling.

"And why is this important to you?" he asked.

He had been listening. She felt excited. "Because I believe we can change what is happening to the world. If we know at what point it shattered — I mean, like when the virus first manifested itself, which is the cause, we can create a new reality — order from the disorder, like the broken glass bottles. The world won't be the same after the virus — think of it as humanity's visit to the brink, hopefully no more than that — we will begin to grow and rebuild again."

"What are you talking about back there? Come on. Catch up, ketchup." Tim laughed at himself. "You know the story of the slow turtle ... I suppose you had to be there."

Ignoring Tim's sick joke Kevin immersed himself in Jade's theory, which was hard to grasp. "We can put humpty dumpty together again, he will just be in a different state of being. Okay, so we can somehow change the global mess we are in if we find out how it all started and fix it."

"Well, yes. Simply put, we have to find the pieces that created the disorder. This didn't just happen. This was the effect of something. We have to change it, put it back some-how." They reached the mountain a few minutes behind the others who were leaning casually on the railing and looking outward. No one was moving.

"What is it?" Kevin asked as he approached his dad, although he didn't need any explanation, because he could see everything from the mountains to the ocean. Most of the waterfront apartments were halved and smoldering. Out at sea, coal ships were on fire and three massive giant demons were forming and unforming, breaking down into smaller versions of themselves into what looked like a flock of birds or a swarm of bees. Nobody moved. Kevin felt like he was in a cyclops movie. Instead of dumb and clumsy, these were an intelligent negative life force of death, an abomination. "A fresh southerly wind is blowing north-east. That's why we weren't getting any smoke," his dad said.

"Look over there, ten o'clock." Tim pointed to the west where the lake met the trees. Five figures, all men, stepped from two four-wheel drive vehicles. Tim handed the binoculars to Kevin.

"What do you think they're doing?" Jade asked. "If we wave, do you believe that we can get their attention? I can barely see them."

"We don't want them to see us," Kevin said.

"Why not?"

Shaun took the binoculars from Kevin. "He's right," Shaun said and handed the binoculars to Daniel. In the distance, the car door slammed silently. Daniel peered through the glasses and could see clearly, as if the five men were mere yards away. One reached into the back of the car and dragged someone out, throwing him to the edge of the lake. Seconds later, Jade drew in a sharp breath. Gunfire echoed across the valley.

"Don't look," Daniel said, but it was too late. Shaun pulled the binoculars back off Daniel. Unsure of what they had just seen, not wanting to believe it, they were rooted to the spot and watched the men get back into the vehicle. They drove off, revealing the actual carnage.

"What did you see?" Kevin asked Shaun. Shaun didn't say anything. "What did you see?"

Shaun had his arm outstretched offering the binoculars to Daniel, but Kevin grabbed them.

"No!" Daniel said.

Kevin held the glasses to his eyes. The crimson shoreline was littered with dead bodies. The water gently lapped up against them. Kevin dropped the glasses and doubled over, his hands on his knees. His legs felt shaky, his stomach did a backflip and turned and turned and turned. He couldn't hold it any longer and his breakfast splattered over the ground.

"Tim, Shaun, get away from the edge." The four-wheel drives had stopped. One person stepped out onto the side rim with his own pair of binoculars and was looking in their direction.

"Guys, quickly, get away from the edge and hide," Daniel said, pushing them down. They made their way back to the pathway and lay down on the ground.

"I think they may have seen the glint of the sun on the lenses," Jade said.

Kevin had never seen so many dead people. "Normal people like you and me. Families dead for what? Nothing." He wiped his mouth and felt the blood moving through his veins again.

"Do you think they saw us?" Tim asked.

"I'm not sure. We'll just wait here until they move on," Daniel said.

The binoculars were where Kevin had dropped them and Shaun started to slither across the ground to get them. Daniel yelled at Shaun to get back. He kept going. He handed the binoculars to Daniel and said, "How long do you think it would take them to get to us from over there?"

Daniel carefully moved into the scrub beside the path and peered down, across the valley to the lake. He saw the men were moving again. "If they wanted to get to us they could be here in an hour."

"But it took us that long to walk up here," Jade said.

"Then we'd better run," Shaun said.

They headed down the path, out into the car park and started jogging down the narrow winding road. Kevin kept pace with Jade and Tim. Shaun and Daniel led the way. Jade held her side.

"You okay?" Kevin asked, jogging beside her.

"Just … just a stitch in my side."

Tim skidded on the gravel as he turned off the road, grazing his leg. Jade and Kevin helped him up. Daniel looked over his shoulder and saw Tim on the ground and ran back. "You okay?"

"Fair dinkum, what did I do? I must have killed a thousand people in a past life."

"Well, actually, "Jade said, panting, "if you believe in karma … then I would say you must have done something right because you haven't been vaporized, crushed, beaten to death, shot, or even swallowed up by *that*," she said, pointing to the east. "So you're doing pretty well. Wouldn't you say?" Jade stopped talking and rested on her knees trying to catch her breath.

"Dust yourself off, mate, it's just a scratch," Daniel said.

They headed off the road and across the paddock. The house was in sight and looked just as they had left it. The road was clear, no dust in the air. All was quiet.

Shaun came up to the wire fence that stretched across the paddock and held the barbed wire down for them all to climb over. It was his turn and Shaun hesitated; Kevin pulled the barbed wire down as far as he could to show him it was okay and there wasn't going to be a surprise attack.

They jumped the white fence onto his grandparent's property. The house was peaceful. Mixed smells of cooking and laugher filtered from the kitchen window, and waiting to greet them on the back veranda was Alex. His dad sighed with relief as he laid his hand on the screen door and Alex's head before picking him up and opening the door fully. He stopped before stepping across the threshold.

"Okay, guys," Daniel said. "Someone needs to always be at the far corner of the front veranda, it's the best view of the approaching road." Alex put his little hand on Daniel's chin and turned his head towards him. "What's happening, Daddy?"

"Nothing, Alex. Go tell your mother we're back." He put Alex down. He watched him run along the hallway with his hand under his armpit trying to blow out a tune.

"No mention of what was on the shoreline, and tonight we will need to reduce the amount of lights. Go around the outside of the house and take the bulbs out of the sensors. If you see a light on in the house turn it off. Make sure all blinds are closed. Keep the noise down and we should take turns during the night watching the road for approaching lights, just in case. Any questions?"

"Yeah, why don't we just get the hell out of here?" Tim asked.

"There isn't anywhere else to go."

KEVIN COULD HEAR, inside the house, Kath and Molly laughing at Alex who was making sounds from his armpits. The smile on his mother's face disappeared as he walked through the kitchen doorway. She looked at his dad, Shaun, Tim and Jade, then back at Kevin.

"You look like you all ran back. Is everything okay?"

He challenged his own urge to hide and pretend she wasn't seeing their worry. "You're right, mom," he said.

"Oh, God, what happened, who's dead?"

Daniel looked at Callie, and then back to Kevin.

We must look to him as if we're having a silent conversation. But I've said nothing, she just knows.

Her hand went to her mouth and she turned back to the sink. Her voice was a little shaky. "Okay, we have made a jug of lemon juice. There was an old cake packet in the cupboard that was only out of date by three months. It will be out of the oven in five minutes. Clean yourselves up, then we can talk about what you all saw."

Kevin moved to the sink and without turning around she said, "Not here, all of you upstairs."

Kevin waited until everyone had gone upstairs before he looked up and down the hallway. The kitchen smelt wonderful from the fresh chocolate cake baking in the oven, and the sound of laughter mixed with lemongrass and sage. He could see out the front door and out the back door, both leading onto the veranda. A gentle breeze banged the back door, which hadn't quite latched. "Nanna, are you here?" He stood still using his peripheral vision and caught a whisper of light that passed him by.

"I knew you were here keeping a watch. Ask God to send the crows and let us know if anyone approaches, please." He breathed in and closed his eyes, breathed out.

"Kevin, who are you talking to?" Callie asked, stepping into the hallway.

What do I say? Kevin opened his eyes, meeting his mother's. "Nanna."

"I feel her too."

Cautiously, he asked, "Can you smell her?"

"What does she smell like to you?"

"Lemongrass and sage."

"Is that so? I've been smelling sage since we arrived,"

Callie smiled. The oven beeped, the cake was ready. For a moment, they stood there awkwardly.

She's changing. "I'm going upstairs," Kevin said and walked off after the others. He stopped at the top of the landing and looked out the arched window. The road was clear.

2

EXTRACTION: SHAUN. AUSTRALIA

Shaun could hear Jade in the next room, crying. He tried to ignore it. Something else had woken him. He looked over at Alex and the little fellow was snoring. The bedside digital clock in bright red announced it was 4:44 a.m. Shaun threw back the sheet and sat on the edge of the bed, mopping his brow. He was covered in perspiration again. He had been dreaming of Rachel and they were in a cave. She had grown into a young woman, standing fearlessly before a giant blazing black dog surrounded by a firestorm. It swiped at her, stabbing her with its claws. He could still feel the heat as he had tried to save her. Then something woke him up.

He pulled on his jeans, quietly opened the door and stopped and listened. He went into Kevin and Tim's room. Tim was snoring and Kevin was half hanging out of the bottom bunk. Shaun then looked into Jade and Kath's room, where Kath was fast asleep, oblivious to Jade's sobbing. He gently poked Jade in the shoulder, trying not to startle her awake. Her eyes shot open, and she stared with a lack of recognition. He had seen that look a thousand times in his father's eyes, but it didn't last long with Jade. She looked puzzled.

"You were crying in your sleep," he whispered, as Kath started to stir. Moonlight was streaming into the room.

Jade looked out the window; a crow crashed into the glass and she gave a little shriek. "Crows don't fly at night," she said, alarmed.

Kath woke in fright and screamed. Shaun slapped his hand over Kath's mouth, frightening her. She struggled and bit his hand.

"What the fuck? Shut up or you're going to wake everyone in the house." Then headlights probed the blackness of the room. "Oh, shit! Jade, go wake Kevin and Tim."

"Kath, get your mom and meet us in Kevin's room. You've got about thirty seconds."

His bare feet slapped the wooden floor as he ran down the empty hallway. He ducked into his room, lifted Alex out of bed and carried him as best he could, although the boy's dangling feet kicked him in the groin. He struggled with the door handle. Alex seemed to weigh a ton, but finally the knob turned and he entered Daniel and Callie's room. Shaun gently tossed Alex in the middle of the bed.

"What's going on?" Daniel said, trying to open his eyes, reaching for the side lamp.

"Don't turn it on, we have company. I just saw their headlights coming up the road."

"Shit, go wake everyone."

"I already have and told them to meet us in Kevin's room."

Alex nestled into Callie, peacefully drifting in and out of sleep. She soothed him, keeping him calm. She moved him aside to climb out of bed, quickly dress and slip into her sneakers. Shaun ran back down the hall to Kevin's room.

Daniel carried Alex, and Callie had Molly in her arms. Shaun reached out for Kevin's doorknob. He hesitated, listening to the sound of tyres moving along the dirt and stone driveway. It was getting closer and stopped somewhere out front.

Quickly, he slipped into Kevin's room. Alex started to whimper in Daniel's arms. Molly was asleep and Callie gently rocked her willing her to stay that way. The car doors opened ... they all held their breaths.

"Shh, you have to stop crying," Shaun said to Alex. "If they hear you crying they will come and hurt us."

"Don't talk like that to my brother. We don't know who they are," Kevin said.

"Yes, we do. It's those guys we saw pop a cap into that dude by the river yesterday. They are also the same guys who chased you and Tim."

"What, no way. Shouldn't we do something? We can't just hide in here," Kevin whispered.

"You saw what they did to that guy?" Now an inch away from Kevin's nose he said. "Didn't you?"

AT SIX IN the evening Casey was slouched in the armchair and started to toss and turn as he dozed. He was burning up. He called out Sophia's name.

"What's happening, is he sick? Why won't he wake up?" said Amy.

"He's okay. I could go into a trance and help him, but this — he has to do this one on his own. If I was meant to be with him, we wouldn't be having this conversation."

Casey's head hung over the side of the chair at an odd angle. Joe picked him up and laid him on the sofa.

Sophia held Casey's hand and the room around them started to change. "Relax, Casey, just relax. We're with you. Don't be afraid, you are here with us." There was a circle of light forming around them and she saw Amy become alarmed and agitated. Sophia wasn't shocked, she knew what was happening. The ghosts of the past started to appear and the apparitions and emotional memories began to play themselves out for all to see. Sophia couldn't help feeling excited; she was thrilled and touched by the display of memories, and the reality of the promise of the afterlife. She had always felt the gentle touch of a world beyond her sight. Father McDonald pulled out his Bible, and started praying for Casey's protection, just as he had done for Sophia throughout her life.

Amy brushed back Casey's hair and blew a cool breeze onto his brow. The apparitions took stronger physical form than previously. She became afraid for Casey. "My book," Amy said, "my grandfather's book."

Sophia saw Amy's fear. "Don't be afraid. No matter what happens he will be okay, even if he dies."

"How can you say that?" Amy said.

"Because it's true. There is an angel that only answers to God that keeps watch over Casey. But he won't die again, not today."

Amy knelt on the floor by the sofa and knocked her knee on something; she pulled a book from under the couch. Sophia was in awe of the light radiating from it. Amy opened the book and the letters glittered and danced off the page. Sophia felt jubilant, astonished and totally amazed.

"Amy, you are holding a book of splendor, a channel to the creator. You are blessed." Tears pooled in her eyes as she looked at Amy, who looked as innocent as a child sitting on the floor. The letters circled and expanded to include every-one. It was a spectacular sight.

"How can I be blessed when I am surrounded by such turmoil, and I am filled with anguish for the pain of human-ity? I have no family. I have lost children before they were born. I am terrified I will lose Casey and he will fall victim, like so many, to the darkness."

Sophia didn't answer. She had no words to express the love Amy amplified with her words.

"Tell me, how can I possibly be blessed?" Amy asked again.

THE WINDOWS WERE CLOSED, the white blinds were drawn. Shaun saw Callie look at Kevin and Tim sitting on the bottom bunk with Jade in between them. Nobody was doing anything. *What are they waiting for?* Shaun thought. *Why are they just sitting around, don't they get it?* Alex was bravely holding back his sobs and buried his face into Daniel's neck and wrapped his legs tight around his waist. Daniel paced the floor. Molly continued to sleep in Callie's arms, unaware of the commotion. "She's always been a good sleeper. Once darkness falls, she dependably sleeps till sunrise," Callie said to Kath.

"We can sneak out the back to the car, or we could make a run for it into the hills," Daniel said.

"Can't we just hide?" Sally said, pulling Kath close to her.

"They will eventually find us," Callie said. They heard the car doors opening and closing.

"I'm not hiding anywhere," Shaun said. "Those guys won't think twice about offing us."

Callie held Molly close to her chest. "I know, follow me!" She left no room for protests. She opened the door, checked the corridor, and was out of the room and rushing down the hallway.

"What the hell, Callie?"

"Daniel, hurry up," she whispered.

The kids jumped up and squeezed past Daniel and Alex. Shaun, Kevin, Tim and Jade ran down the back stairs after her. She went out the back and onto the veranda. Quietly, in the dark, they slithered along the side wall of the house towards the hangar. There was only fifteen feet between the house and the hangar's side door, but it might as well have been a mile. Callie had stopped. Shaun heard the front door splintering as it yielded to the pressure of heavy boots. He felt a chill rush up his spine. He saw Callie clutch Molly even tighter. Suddenly she ran into the opening making a dash for the hangar. Kevin raced past Callie and he reefed the side door open and they all piled in.

Lastly, Daniel ushered Sally and Kath into the hangar. The door quietly clicked closed behind them. "What are you thinking, Cal?" Daniel whispered.

"We can fly out of here. Isn't it obvious?"

"The plane hasn't been started for over a year — and what about those things in the sky? It's filled with them."

"These guys are going to —"

Before she could finish there was a flash of light streaming from the house. The hangar's only window lit up. Suddenly there was a loud bang. *Gunfire*, Shaun thought.

"Come out, come out, wherever you are." The stranger's voice was loud and sinister.

Callie reached for the plane's keys. Daniel moved Alex onto his hip and stepped up onto the wing. With one hand he held the door open. "Come on, everyone. Quick. It is going to be a tight squeeze," he said.

Callie stopped Kevin before they climbed up onto the wing. "You have to help me. You're the only person who has flown this plane."

"What? Me!" Kevin protested. "Pop only gave me a couple of lessons."

"Just about the same as me," Callie said. "You remember the walk-around checks? Remove the tie-downs, check the fuel, tyres, remove the cover from ... what's it called?"

"The Pitot tube. Shit, Ma."

"I'm not getting in there if he's flying," Shaun said.

Callie raised her eyebrows. "You have to."

"Kevin! Stop underestimating yourself. Now move."

He stood smiling at her positive words, which didn't elude him.

"Why are you smiling? Move."

Kevin hurried to begin the external procedures. Callie jumped up into the cockpit. Shaun climbed in after her and watched her start the pre-flight checklist. *This is going to take forever.*

KEVIN SEARCHED the empty bench drawers for the clear flask to do the fuel check. "Top drawer, K," he imagined his pop saying. The Piper Cherokee 6-300 had been sitting unused in the hangar for over a year. Kevin wasn't sure that it would even start, but first there had to be fuel and it had to be unspoilt. He could hear gunshots as the men searched through the house, randomly firing like idiots. He had to relax, he had to concentrate. There was a lot of ifs in front of them. Relax, Kevin told himself, and the image of his first night flight six years ago when he was eight came into his mind. The yellow and white streetlights below had been beautiful. It had looked as if the city was wrapped up in glittery gold and silver tinsel. He fell in love with flying that night. The gunfire brought him back to the present. *What the hell? Daydreaming now, K, is going get you killed.*

He found a torch and a tube and walked over to the plane, draining about an inch of fuel out of each wing. He first smelt it; the potency smacked him in the face. He then checked the color and clarity of the mix and, to his surprise, it was perfect. He checked the tanks: the left wing was full, the right side not so much. He continued the procedure, remembering how much he loved flying. He nearly jumped out of his skin when gunfire echoed through the house. He kicked the tyre blocks out of the way and climbed up onto the wing. It all took no more than couple of minutes, but it felt like an eternity.

"Left wing's up to taps," he said to his mom.

He looked into the back of the small plane; it only had four passenger seats. Next to Jade, Alex was sitting on his dad's lap. Sally was cradling Molly, sitting beside Kath. Tim climbed over the white leather seats into the baggage space and nestled in the rear fuselage behind Jade. Shaun sat on the floor between the four seats. Kevin suddenly felt his eyes well up and his throat tighten with tears, then realized they weren't his tears, weren't his emotions, they were Jade's. He smiled at Jade, then looked at his mom. "There's no room in the back for me," he said.

She patted the co-pilot seat. "I reserved it for you." She resumed going through the pre-flight checklist; he could see the aileron and the flaps on the wings going up and down. He moved to his seat and put on his headset. Callie handed him the laminated checklist and he read out the next instruction.

"Carburetor heat — off."

"Check." His mom's voice came through his speakers loud and clear.

"Annunciator panel — check lights."

"Check."

"Circuit breakers — check in."

"Throttle — ¼ inch open."

"Check."

"Mixture — rich."

"Check."

"Fuel pump — on."

"Check."

"Primer —"

"Callie," Kath said, her face butted up against the small side panel posing as a window. Her voice was quivering. "How much longer is this going to take? I can see them. Do you think they know we are here? The house is lit up like a power plant. They are going to kill us, aren't they? They're going through every room. Three of the men are heading onto the veranda."

Daniel placed his hand on Callie's shoulder, his voice controlled, totally monotone. "I don't think we have time for this, Cal."

Kevin and Callie ignored them, concentrating on the procedures.

"Okay, I don't want to open the hangar until we have started the engine," she said. "We are going for a cold engine start. Sorry for stating the obvious."

Kevin nodded and kept reading the pre-flight checks.

"Magnetos — both."

"CLEAR PROP," Kevin shouted, looking out the side panel window.

"Start engine — set 1000 rpm and confirm oil pressure."

And Callie started the engine. The plane coughed and went silent. Callie started the engine again. It coughed — and pulsed into life.

Kevin checked the oil pressure. "Okay, handbrake off," Kevin said and the plane began to move.

"The door! The hangar door!" Daniel yelled.

"Where's the remote?" Callie fumbled in the side pocket of the door where the pre-flight checklist was kept, and blindly searched with her fingers for the remote control. "Got it." She pushed the button. The hangar door groaned, slowly moving and clunking as it folded back into the roof. She lifted her toes off the brakes and onto the rudder.

"Damn, I forgot the specimens." Callie braked hard. "Handing over control," she said into the mike, "You got it, Kevin?" and started to undo her seat belt.

"I have control," he said robotically just like his pop taught him. But he didn't want control, he wanted his mom to take it back. "Where are you going?"

"Taxi out of here and pick me up at the back paddock fence," she said.

"But, Mom —"

"No buts!" In a softer tone, she said, "You can do this, Kevin." Callie climbed onto the wing and slid off the plane.

Daniel yelled at Callie over the sound of the engine. "Where the hell are you going? What could be more important than your family? For Christ's sake... Cal!"

Kevin saw her shoot out from behind the plane, out the side door and she was gone. The hangar door was wide open, and Kevin steered the plane with his feet. Three men suddenly appeared in front of the aircraft and Kevin slammed on the brakes. He idled just before the threshold.

"Get out of the plane," one of them demanded. Their rifles were raised, ready to fire.

"Dad?"

"Floor it, K," Daniel said.

"But, Dad, what if they don't move?"

"Floor it, K, full throttle."

Kevin released the brake and the plane started rolling. Flashes of light ignited from the gun barrels. The bullets ricocheted off the propeller blades. The men didn't budge. Kevin turned the plane as sharply as he could, trying to avoid them, hoping they would duck under the wing, but he felt the sudden shudder of the propeller. There was a yell from inside the house. Callie screamed. They could see her silhouette fighting, struggling with one of the men by the kitchen window.

"Callie!" Daniel screamed and held Alex's head close to his chest blocking his ears.

Kevin screamed out his window for the men to leave her alone. It was impossible for him to be heard. The two men still standing in their way took off and went back into the house. Kevin rolled the plane out of the hangar, towards the front of the house and the two four-wheel drives.

SHAUN WASN'T in the best position to see what was going on outside the plane, but his hearing was just fine. He was cramped, but he felt safe. It had been a long time since he had been on a plane and a long time since he felt safe, but now, hearing Callie's screams, anxiety crawled over him.

The anguish in Daniel's voice as he shouted to Callie was like nails down a chalkboard.

"Oh, God, please, please no." Daniel sat Alex on Jade's lap and reached for the door.

Shaun watched Daniel. He was ready to jump onto the wing and off the plane, but he hesitated. He looked back at them all and Shaun could see, in his eyes, the pain. Shaun knew then that Daniel wouldn't leave them. He sat back down and gripped the cold metal handle, while Kevin taxied in front of the house. Shaun looked up into Daniel's face and saw the torment. He wriggled out of his tight spot and slipped through the partially open door. He felt Daniel grapple for his shirt before he fell onto the wing. Shaun landed hard, grazing himself on the gravel driveway. He jumped up and hid behind the side of the moving plane. Hunched over, he ran to the back of the house. He was out of sight. He no longer heard Daniel yelling at him to get back on board.

He saw Kevin speed down the drive, into the dark, towards the short runway. Shaun stayed down. He had the advantage of surprise and wanted to keep it that way.

"It's the woman. Hold her still."

Shaun snuck up the back steps. Then he stopped, and remembered the can of petrol under the workbench, below where Callie had found the keys. He crept back down the stairs and ran into the hangar and grabbed the can and some rags. Keeping quiet he headed to the front of the house and crouched beside the first four-wheel drive. He popped open the petrol cap and stuffed in the dripping rag, then did the same with the second four-wheel drive. He could hear Callie screaming and it actually bothered him. *When did I start to care? It hurts too much to care.* He couldn't cut off the sound of her screams. *Why did she go back, anyway? For what, a couple of specimen jars?* The doubt was smothering him. *I should just run and not look back. I don't need them.* Ignoring his thoughts he focused on the lighter in his hand and the soaked rags. This was familiar, making petrol bombs, and the feeling of confidence returned. He knew how to blow shit up. Shaun set each rag alight and ran down the side of the house. The explosion threw him off his feet and he could feel the heat over his back and head. He could smell it singeing his hair. He scrambled to his feet as the men ran out the front door.

Shaun ran up the back stairs and through the back door. He stopped in the hallway and peered into the kitchen. Callie was being held by the neck up against the far wall. There was only one man in the room. Shaun picked up the brick that was acting as a doorstopper and rushed at the man, whacking him hard in the back of the head. It took Callie a few seconds to register Shaun, but as soon as she did she was moving, pulling open the refrigerator for her little blue esky.

Shaun gripped her wrist. "Leave it. We have to get out. Come on."

Callie had what she was looking for and was first out the back, the screen door's spring slowly retracting as the door closed gently behind them. They hurdled over the veranda railing and headed across the paddock. Shaun could just make out the flashing red and green lights on the wings of the plane as it turned off the road speeding across the paddock towards them. It slowed, but didn't stop. The cabin door flung open and Daniel grabbed the esky from Callie. She ran next to the plane, stumbled. Daniel leant out and reached for her hand as bullets whistled past their heads. Daniel lifted Callie up into the plane. The men ran across the paddock closing the gap between them. A bullet hit the tail wing. Shaun heard it first pass his ear and he instinctively ducked. The plane was pulling away. They were going to leave him.

Daniel came back out onto the wing. "Run, Shaun, run. Come on, boy, faster."

Shaun dug his toes into the grass and sprinted to catch up. He reached his hand out to Daniel, missed, and touched the flap. He reached up and felt Daniel's hand around his wrist. Shaun tried to climb, his dirty feet slipping, leaving skid marks along the wing. Daniel held the door with one hand and pulled Shaun towards the cabin with the other. Shaun gripped the side of the cabin, practically crawling in through the door and felt a hot poker in his back. He slipped back out onto the wing. The pain quickly became excruciating and swept over his whole body. Daniel had a strong hold and pulled Shaun screaming, up and inside the plane. Shaun lay slumped over Jade and Daniel's lap.

Alex put his hand on his head. "You'll be okay, Shaun."

Shaun felt Alex's little hand on his head patting him as the plane turned and accelerated away from the house. Kevin pushed the throttle all the way up and the plane thrust forward. It seemed to take forever to get into the air and when the tyres left the ground Shaun's stomach suddenly dropped and they were up.

"You're bleeding! Oh, my god, you're bleeding!" Kath said.

He could see ahead between the two front seats as if he was lying on the back seat of a car. Kevin and Callie were pulling back on the yoke, changing the pitch of the plane, as it went higher and higher into the dark sky. *Molly's ears must be aching*, Shaun thought when she let out a piercing scream. Alex sobbed quietly on Jade's lap. Daniel pushed down harder on Shaun's back trying to stop the bleeding.

I've been shot, he wanted to say. *The bullet hasn't come out the other side. It must be lodged in an organ or something.* He was dizzy and didn't feel much of anything any more. He looked at Alex and said, "You're alright ... you'll be fine," and Shaun's eyes closed.

Casey lay on the sofa in Amy's house. The windows were boarded up. The chill of the English air was coming under the doors and down the chimney. Casey could hear Sophia and Amy as they tried to wake him up. Their voices seemed to be a long way away. He was too far from his body to go back now.

Casey could feel the other boy's distress and moved closer towards him until he saw him shudder. A cold chill ran down the boy's spine. *I'm the cold chill*, he thought. Casey endeavored to see where he was and to get a look at him, but he could only see out of the boy's eyes. He was in a plane, that much was obvious. The boy was hot, sticky with sweat and he could feel everyone else's emotional pain. He was peering through the cockpit window into the dark, searching the fields for someone. He spotted a woman, his mother, running from the back of the house and steered the plane straight across the field towards her. A wave of relief washed over him once she was on board and could help fly. Casey felt the boy's surge of gratitude for a boy who was with his mother, when suddenly the other boy was shot in the back.

Casey managed to move from the boy's mind, around the cockpit and out through the windshield to look back at him. *This is so incredible — I've totally left my body. Hey, I know that face, I know that guy!* Casey thought. It was the last thing he remembered seeing a year ago, when he fell from the bridge into the floodwaters.

Casey heard the boy's mother telling him to pull up; they pulled on the controls together lifting the nose up and the plane rising into the air. She called him Kevin — his name is Kevin! They were in the air. Behind them, Casey could see dark clouds heading towards the rear of the plane. It wasn't any ordinary storm. The clouds were controlled; a swarm of evil micro-organisms were chasing them. A few surrounded the engine, so it became totally concealed by what looked like a swarm of bees. It ignited into flames and Kevin and the passengers screamed as the flames lit up the sky.

Why am I seeing this? I am about to witness this kid's death. It was terrible, they had no chance, and the engine was gone. The nose bowed to the earth and gravity did the rest. The girl in the back was yelling at Kevin to open a door. *Why would she want him to open the door?* Casey wondered. There was no point in jumping. Casey slipped back inside Kevin. Kevin's desire to save his family was so overwhelming that Casey felt like he was going to explode with energy. Kevin had become a powerhouse.

The girl leant forward and Casey could hear her as if she was in his own head. "Kevin, listen to me," she said. "Relax, you got this."

Next to Kevin, his mother was fighting with the controls and trying to spin a wheel down at the side of her seat. "Trim, trim," she said, trying to get the nose of the falling plane to lift up. "Trim, damn it. I can't hold it."

Then Kevin relaxed. Casey could feel him relax and his own body, lying on the couch with Sophia and Amy around him, relaxed. *Kevin, can you hear me?* Casey asked. He didn't answer. Casey watched as a small hole started to appear in the atmosphere directly in front of the plane as it jolted and dived. Everyone screamed. Lightning slammed into the tail, taking out the rudder along with Kevin's focus.

Kevin? Casey said.

~

KEVIN STRUGGLED with the controls and thought, *I'm a little busy, if you haven't noticed. I hear you, loud and clear. Get the hell out of my head.* Then suddenly they traded places. Kevin was inside Casey's mind seeing Casey's memories. He could feel a cold cloth on his brow. He was lying on a comfy couch. Casey had been with a girl, laughing and riding a motorcycle. She looked familiar too. Kevin didn't have the mental capacity to focus on her, because his family was about to die. He pulled himself out of Casey's head and back into the cockpit.

Casey could feel Kevin's confusion. You know her, Casey said, don't you? Come here, come to us, come to England.

You're about a thousand miles away and three days too late, Kevin replied. The girl was yelling again for Kevin to open the door. *I know who you are.* Kevin's eyes moved over Casey's memory again, seeing him riding down the driveway lined with birch trees on a chilly English afternoon. He focused on the memory and opened the door. The cockpit was filled with sage and lemongrass and his mouth tasted of metal. A soft hum pulsed through the plane. Lightning exploded, revealing a translucent ripple of energy stretched out in front; an opening, a doorway.

The engine stopped and the sky was filled with silence. The plane continued to fall, dropping into the mirage, vanishing from the sky.

Casey felt heavy, back in his own body on the sofa. He was surrounded by Joe, Terry, Amy, Father McDonald and Sophia. Casey willed his muscles to move; he had to tell Sophia what he had seen. He stirred. It was hard to get control of his own body again, it felt like lead. He started feeling the sofa under his body and Amy changing the wet cloth on his brow. Slowly he opened his eyes. Apparitions in the room were fading as he returned.

"Hey, you," Amy said. "Are you okay?"

Casey tried to slowly prop himself up. His body still felt like it weighed an additional two hundred pounds. He was exhausted, but he needed to talk to Sophia. He needed to tell her before he forgot. He dropped back onto the sofa. His lips were dry and Terry was ready with a glass or water. Casey reached for the glass. Terry held it to Casey's mouth. He took a sip and said. "Sophia, I think it's the others. His name's Kevin."

Father McDonald struggled onto his feet and moved closer to Casey. "Is the boy okay? Who else is with him?"

3

KNIGHTS AT THE LONG TABLE: CASEY.
ENGLAND

Boom! The windows rattled. Outside, a high-pitched, teeth-clenching screech of metal could be heard scraping down the driveway.

Joe was first to the door.

Terry, Amy and Father McDonald, already on their feet, followed Joe. "You two stay here," Amy said, looking at Casey and Sophia. Amy's gaze met Sophia's blue eyes. "Look after him, okay." She left the room.

"You guys!" Joe yelled over his shoulder as he ran out. "It's a plane!" He jumped down the steps following the aircraft and waiting for it to stop sliding.

JUST SHORT OF crashing into the birch trees, the plane lay silent in the twilight. No burst of flames, no smoldering fire. Joe approached with caution. The plane rested, tilted on its side. The left wing had been torn off on impact and lay a yard away from the aircraft. The paint was stripped back, the side sliced open and the tyres had blown out. It was amazing it wasn't a fireball. Joe thought he saw movement from inside the plane. He pushed down and bounced on the right wing testing its stability. Confident it would hold he hoisted himself up. He saw people moving in the darkness of the cabin. He pulled at the door. It wouldn't open, so he dug his nails in between the cracks of the door and the plane and tried to wrench it open. No good. The grass around the belly of the aircraft was starting to smoke a little and he thought he could smell fuel. A baby cried. Someone was kicking at the door. The plane rolled a bit more onto its belly, tilting further to the left and flames ignited in the grass. The banging against the door grew stronger. Joe pulled and pulled at the door. Everything was happening too fast.

Terry came up next to Joe with a crowbar in hand. "Okay, Joe. Together!"

Both men leant their weight against the wedged bar and the door strained and popped open. A baby coughing, choking on its own tears was handed to Joe. He passed the little bundle down to Amy, and she quickly walked away from the plane to safety. Next was a young boy. Terry lowered him to the ground. Father McDonald took the boy's hand and together they rushed to Amy. The plane's tail ignited.

"Mommy, Daddy!" the young boy cried. He was pulling at Father McDonald's hand trying to go back to help.

Joe held his hand out to each person emerging from the plane and guided them off the wing. Two teenage girls, two women, one gripping a white and blue icebox, two boys, and the man who had kicked the door dragged an unconscious young man out onto the wing. Joe's eyes were tearing with smoke.

"Joe, move back," Terry yelled.

Joe jumped off the wing and the man dragged the boy to the edge of the wing and climbed down. He grabbed the young man under his armpits and pulled.

"Grab his legs," he yelled to Joe.

Together they carried and laid him on the ground next to the coughing boys. Joe expected the plane to blow any second. Amy took the two women and children into the house. Joe scrambled after Terry to grab a hose, and shovels. "We have to get this fire under control before it burns the surrounding trees." Joe dragged the hose across to the plane, passing the passengers taking refuge against the house, and saw the unconscious young man was sitting up. Terry was firing foam onto the burning aircraft.

"Where did you get that from?" Joe asked.

"It was in the boot of the SUV," Terry yelled back.

The man and one of the boys picked up the shovels and tossed dirt from the driveway onto the fuselage. Joe turned the nozzle and a stream of water flowed.

The man yelled at him to stop.

"Not water! It will just spread the fuel." He sat the boy back down against the house and jogged over to Joe. "Let it burn itself out."

Joe turned off the nozzle and Terry finished emptying the fire extinguisher.

A boy with a button nose and auburn hair hanging in his eyes stood next to Joe and said, "Hi, thanks for that. The plane looks like it's ready for a shave, don't you think? Fair dinkum, we're lucky. We've made a hell of a mess of your yard. That will be Kevin's fault," he said, pointing to the athletic-looking chap.

Joe smiled. The odd young man walked off over to his friend and smacked him on the back and side by side they watched the smoldering flames.

Joe, rubbing dirt off his hands, walked up to the man and Terry and said, "Where are you from? Your accents tell me you're not from around here. If I was to take a stab in the dark, I'd say you're from that land down under. Aye, well, you're best to be moving inside."

Terry shook Daniel's hand and said, "I'm Terry. That was Joe. Come in and get yourselves cleaned up."

Joe walked up the back stairs into the kitchen and leant his elbows on the sink. He turned on the tap, and allowed the water to pool in his cupped hands, splashing the water onto his face. He gave the soap to Terry, before pulling paper towels off the wall mount to pat his face and hands dry. He sized up the newcomers who had literally dropped out of the sky.

The woman, late thirties, shoulder-length sandy blonde hair, hiding behind glasses that gave her a dull, slightly old-fashioned look, was clutching a wee icebox under one arm and held the girl baby in the other.

She stood up and moved to the fridge. "Can we put this in your freezer?" she asked, and reluctantly handed over the tiny icebox. Amy smiled and obliged, moving a few items to make space.

"What the hell?" Joe tossed the wet paper towels in the garbage. He moved smoothly, considering his size, around the kitchen table, nearly knocking Amy off her feet as she closed the refrigerator door. The eldest boy from the plane had a large patch of fresh blood on the back of his shirt. It was soaked. His shirt was torn and burnt around the tear, a bullet hole. The boy followed Joe's gaze and tried to crank his neck around to look at himself. Joe pulled up his shirt to find the source of the bleeding. The icebox woman handed the baby to one of the teenagers and joined Joe's search of the boy's back. But there was nothing there.

She held the boy's shoulders and said, "What were you thinking!" She pulled him in for a hug. He had no chance to pull away. "Thank you," she said, "but don't you ever do that again."

The man holding the little lad also embraced the young man.

"Okay, it was nothing. Don't sweat." Embarrassed, he stepped out of the embrace.

The other young lad with the sooty face — who was trying to hide behind his fringe — looked up and said, "Yeah, thanks, man."

"You did it, K. You did it," the girl said softly.

No one seemed badly hurt, a few bumps and bruises. *They can't be all one family.*

"Nice flying, dude. Fair dinkum, I thought we were on our way to meet my dad. I was shitting myself," his button-nosed pal said, patting him on the back.

But what the hell does fair dinkum mean? Joe thought.

Terry cleared his throat and began the introductions. Joe was impressed by his host and hostess who were now unflinchingly welcoming these new people into their home. It was hardly forty-eight hours since they let Sophia, Father McDonald and himself take refuge.

In a strong Aussie accent the man shook Terry's hand and arm and said, "I'm Daniel, thanks a million. I wouldn't have been able to open the door without you and your crowbar. This is my wife Callie, and our baby Molly. This is Sally and her two children, Tim and Kath. That's Jade, Shaun and my two sons, Alex and —"

Joe turned at the utterly unexpected sound of Sophia and Casey's voices in unison saying, "Kevin."

Everyone turned in the direction of the living room. Standing on the threshold, half-hidden by shadows, were

Sophia and Casey. Kevin wiped his eyes against his shoulders, pushing his fringe to one side to see clearly. Confused, he stepped forward. *What the hell?*

Casey and Sophia stepped forward into the light and Kevin stopped as if he recognized Casey. He turned to his mother to say something and stopped.

"How do you know my name?" Kevin asked.

The atmosphere in the room had changed. Everyone was mystified and wanted to know.

"Sophia talked about you. You recognize her, don't you?"

Kevin looked nervously at his mother and father and then at his friend, who shrugged his shoulders.

"Yeah, I remember her. She was there that day, when you fell. You fell into the river."

Joe caught glimpses of confusion, affection and shame from Kevin's parents.

"How the hell did you survive?" Kevin said. "How?"

"Yeah?" Tim said, stepping around the table and standing by Kevin. "He got into so much shit trying to help you that day. Everyone thought he was a crazy attention-seeker." Tim raised his hands and made exclamation marks with his fingers. "The boy who cried wolf."

Jade stepped forward too and stood next to Tim. It was starting to look a little like a showdown.

"Okay, people," the young lass said, "I think we should be focusing on why we are all connected? Why are we *all* here?" She moved forward and introduced herself to Casey and Sophia. "I'm Jade."

Then she shifted uncertainly from one foot to the other, looking down at her feet, as if deciding whether to speak further or not. She chose not to speak and stepped back. Kevin looked at her as if he couldn't quite work her out. *She's a strange wee hen*, Joe thought. *One minute she was shy, the next outgoing and taking control.*

"She's right," Father McDonald said. "Sophia has been prepared for .... I don't fully understand what, but the time is now. For these young ones to know each other is a miracle. You just survived a plane crash and that's a miracle, and for none of us to be sick with the virus is another miracle. God has protected us with his armor."

Then, in a faint voice, Kevin heard Shaun say, "And I took a bullet in the back and only have a bloody shirt, is a miracle."

Terry said. "You're welcome to stay as long as you like."

JOE HELPED Amy prepare the house for her new guests. He carried the linen to her great-aunt's old room downstairs, which was for Daniel, his wife and his two young ones.

"This room has an en suite and the bed should be big enough for you all," Amy said, showing Callie the room. "If you'd like a cot, there is one in the basement. The men can bring it up, so just ask."

Joe laid the fresh towels and linen on the bed.

"That won't be necessary, thank you," Callie said.

"The three boys can share with Casey. It's a massive room and is right above you. Upstairs, next to the main bathroom, is Sophia's room and Jade can bunk with her. The room is across and down the hall a little from the boys. Father McDonald and Joe are next to Sophia's room. Sally and her daughter will be further down the hall in the old nursery. Once you've freshened up, please join us in the living room for some tea." Amy left Callie with her little boy and baby. Exhausted, Amy went and sat down in the living room.

Joe followed her. He was struck by her caring nature; he couldn't take his eyes off her. She picked up her black book and held it open in her lap and started to read. He wasn't sure if she knew he was there. He cleared his throat and she closed the book in fright.

"Oh, sorry Joe, you gave me a fright. I didn't hear you come in."

"Amy, I want to thank you."

"For what, Joe? I haven't done anything that you yourself wouldn't have done. Why don't we go and help Terry and you could slice up some of that delicious boiled date cake you made. I think I am going to like this."

"What's that?" Joe asked.

"Two men in the house who love to cook."

It wasn't long before Kevin, Tim and Jade came downstairs, refreshed and hungry. Casey and Sophia sat alone at the far end of the white kitchen table that seated twelve. Terry was at the kitchen bench wiping the side of a teapot with his tea towel, and Joe was slicing up two cakes.

Kevin pulled out a white chair and sat opposite Casey and Sophia. Jade decided to sit at the head of the table in between them like an adjudicator.

"You saw me that day," Kevin said to Casey.

"You were the last thing I saw above the surface of the water, when I was pulled under for the last time."

"What do you mean, pulled under?" Tim asked.

"I felt something. The water went murky and I felt as if a claw had wrapped around my leg. It held me and dug its nails into my calf muscle, and my knee was wedged between the rocks. It was pretty mangled when Terry found me. I was lying on a road a mile away from the creek, in the middle of a freak hurricane."

"That wasn't a creek, that was a raging river," Kevin said.

"It was a creek earlier that morning, a dried-up creek."

"What happened between the time you were being pulled under and when you were found on the road?" Jade asked, resting her chin in her hand, leaning forward as if intrigued with Casey's story. Kevin couldn't help smiling as he watched her.

"I don't know. Suddenly I was on the road in the middle of a storm spewing up muddy water and hearing a panicked voice telling me it's going to be all right. That was Terry, and I have been with them ever since."

"What about your parents?" Jade asked, sitting back.

"Dead." Casey lowered his head and traced the lines on the table before looking back at Jade.

"You worry about your mom," Sophia said to Jade as Joe gave her a piece of cake. "Thanks, Joe."

"How? How do you know that? You don't know me." Jade became defensive.

"No, I don't, but it governs your aura. You care for her; you believe Kevin is the key."

Feeling the emotions and tension escalating between the two girls, Kevin moved in his seat uncomfortably.

"We all have something, a gift, and that's why we are together," Sophia said.

"Okay, peeps, cards on the table," Tim said. "Am I the only non-gifted person here? I suppose that makes me unique — extraordinary, as a matter of fact."

Kevin rolled his eyes, smiled and nudged him in the side. "Chill."

"Dude, really? My ribs are killing me from the last time you elbowed me," Tim said. "And let's not mention the plane crash."

"Guys, if you want to hug, go ahead. They are always like this," Jade said, looking at Joe as he put the cake on the table next to cutlery and plates for everyone.

Joe smiled at her and said, "I was like that with my brother. I would love to have been free enough to just hug him." He walked out into the living room.

"Okay, what do we do? Who goes first?" Kevin could feel a sense of urgency from Casey and Sophia.

Sophia pulled her chair a little closer to the table, leant forward and said in a soft voice, "We need to return something. I have seen images of caves and statues. But I don't know what has to be returned. I'm hoping one of you know."

They looked at each other: Tim at Kevin and Kevin at Jade, Jade at Casey and Sophia. Casey kept looking at Jade.

"What, why are you focused on me?" she said.

"Your energy is connected to whatever it is, and don't ask me how I know, I just see it around you."

"When I touched her ..." Kevin ran his fingers through his fringe, pushing back his hair as he moved in his seat, becoming uncomfortable. He worried what he was about to say would be misinterpreted. "What I mean is, when I helped her up, I felt a strong connection, and there was a surge of energy that raced through my body. I felt like it was uniting us. Jade is crucial. Then I find out she knows my mom, and my mom knows her mom, and my mom was the last person to see her mom."

"Think about your mom, Jade," Sophia said and closed her eyes. Sophia's breathing started to slow.

Kevin could sense that Jade was scared and she folded her arms across her chest. "I'm waiting for the crystal ball to appear," she said. "I suppose it's in the cupboard with the shackles and the sheets for a ghost. This is like a carnival sideshow." She was trying hard not to burst into nervous laughter. Sophia spoke, sending shivers down Jade's spine.

"The Indian knows ... your mom's not dead ... Great Turtle said she's not in the spirit world."

"Stop it!" Jade pushed back her chair and stepped away from the table. She looked at Kevin to back her up.

He could feel her panic. She wanted to believe, but her logic was keeping her suspicious and confused. He gave her the most innocent look of support and kindness. She zeroed in on Tim instead and punched him in the arm.

"Why me? That's it!" Tim said. "No more violence! We are up to our necks in this crappy world because of violence; no more. Next person that hits me is going to get ..." Tim chewed his lip, looked up for an answer. "I don't know what, but I'll come up with something non-violent!"

Jade went cherry-red. "Sorry, Tim, I just want it to be true." She started crying and Sophia went to her and hugged her. "I'm sorry."

Jade shoved Sophia into a chair and held her down by the shoulders. "Don't hug me, I don't know you. I want it to be true, I want it to be true so much, please tell me it's true." Jade turned away from the table and leant against the sink.

"It's true. I don't know where she is, but she's not dead." Sophia reached for the tea pot.

Tim picked up the knife and started cutting more cake and passed everyone a second piece. No one spoke. They sipped tea and picked at the cake. Tim was finished within three bites and had a third piece. Kevin watched his friend and could feel his light energy. Tim, unknowingly, had changed the atmosphere, clearing the heaviness that Jade's emotions created in the room. Kevin gave his mate a half smile and raised his eyebrows.

"Well, if we don't know what it is that has to be put back," Kevin said, "how do we find out?"

"Someone will know," Sophia said.

"But none of us know," Casey said.

"Someone knows," Sophia said again.

Joe walked into the kitchen and leant over Kevin to cut a piece of cake, excusing himself as he did. "If she says someone will know, you ought to believe her." Joe scraped a wooden chair over the floor as he pulled it out and sat at the table. "She told me that we would find this place. We were walking underground in the dark, and here we are." He stuffed the piece of cake into his mouth, pushed back the chair, and walked out.

"I like that man," Tim said. "I think we are from the same loaf."

"Okay, then," Casey said, watching Kevin chew his fingernails. "The man's got a point."

Jade pushed off the sink, picked a napkin off the table to wipe her eyes and sat down in her chair, still trying to process the information. She started twisting the napkin. "Is he a Buddhist?" she said softly. "Jewish, Hindu or Kabbalist? The red string? Is it to realign his energy, a symbol of prayer, to bring people together, or is it a sign of protection and goodwill? You have one too, Sophia."

"Are you going to keep guessing the answers to your own questions, or would you like me to jump in?" Sophia asked.

Jade blushed again. "Please, sorry."

Sophia twirled her red string and touched her medallion under her shirt and looked thoughtful, before saying, "You should ask Joe. But it does, it does all those things."

"Tell them what you know," Casey said to Sophia.

Kevin couldn't take his eyes off Casey. He still couldn't believe it was actually him — and he was alive. "Where were you when you drowned?"

"In Utah, USA."

"I thought I recognized your accent, but why do you two sound different?" Tim asked, referring to Jade.

"We are from different parts of the States, approximately two thousand miles apart," Jade said.

"How did you get here?" Kevin asked.

"Amy's great-aunt left her this place. We came over just before the borders closed and flights were grounded. We have been stuck here ever since."

"So how do you know each other?" Kevin said to Casey.

Sophia and Casey looked at each other and Sophia said, "After I saw him drowning, I kept an eye on him."

"How?" Tim asked. "You have an unmistakable Scottish accent."

"I can astral travel."

"You can what?"

"Astral travel. I was, am, a disturbed kid. I miss my dead family and wanted to be with them so much I separated my spirit from my body, and astral traveled. I have to be asleep or in a deep meditative state. Is that how you saw Casey in the river?" she asked Kevin.

"Well, no, I was wide awake when I popped up in the middle of the river."

"We're getting off the subject here," Casey said. He turned to Sophia and expressed in a hushed tone, "If you think we are supposed to be in this together, you'd better tell them what you know."

"Hang on, hang on, everybody," Tim said. "The question is," he said, pointing to Kevin and Jade, "where are we now?"

"What do you mean?" Casey asked.

Father McDonald walked in from outside. "Sophia, it's time. You need to inform the adults."

Sophia stood up and Father McDonald put his arm around her shoulders, more for her help rather than her comfort. The others without a word got out of their chairs and followed them into the living room.

"Where are we?" Tim watched them leave. "I asked one question."

4

WINDOWS IN TIME: ENGLAND

Shaun opened the door and steam rushed from the en suite.

"You will pass out in there if you have it too hot," Callie said.

"I want Shaun to stay with me," Alex said with a little boy's enthusiasm.

"No, Alex. Shaun will want to go in with the big boys."

"I don't want to go to sleep," Alex said, jumping up on the bed, then jumping onto Shaun's back as he passed. Shaun didn't anticipate the move, and staggered about, then spun around playfully before dropping backwards onto the bed.

"Body slam," Alex said.

Shaun had never had a younger brother and wasn't sure how to behave. He preferred to scare little kids, so they would stay clear. Alex was persistent and wasn't easily scared. "I don't mind," Shaun said. "I'll stay with Alex until he goes to sleep."

"Yeah, yahoo!" Alex was thrilled and jumped up and down on the bed.

"Alex, shh, Molly's asleep. Shaun can only stay if you promise to be quiet and get in bed." He bounced down onto his butt and scrambled under the blankets.

"Move over," Shaun said.

"Okay," Callie said. "Shaun, when he's asleep, come into the living room."

"No worries," Shaun said.

Shaun made himself comfortable and began to tell Alex a story his mother had once told him about a boy with magical balloons tied to the post of his bed. When night fell and everyone else was asleep, he would untie the balloons and they would take him on a magical journey across the world, returning him before sunrise. Alex fell asleep before the balloon boy's journey ended and he returned from the heart of Africa. Shaun slid off the bed and quietly left the room, closing the door gently behind him. He quickly stepped across the foyer, avoiding the others, and headed straight upstairs to his room.

"How did we get here? Your guess is as good as mine," Daniel said to Terry.

Daniel placed his cup of tea on the side table as Sophia and the others entered the room. Tired, they plonked themselves on the floor and leant against the furniture.

"We were going down," Daniel continued. "The engine was on fire and it stalled. Time seemed to stop: everything went quiet, muffled, the plane levelled. Sound returned and again we were falling, the craft screaming with the acceleration. Callie and Kevin pulled the nose up seconds before we nose-dived into the ground. My question is, how did we survive?"

"Over the last week we have seen things that are just not of this world, and we have experienced the absolute impossible," Callie said.

"Miracles ..." Father McDonald cleared his throat. "You're experiencing miracles. You have been chased by the servants of hell. Your cars collided at the front of the farmhouse you escaped to. Next you're in a plane running from some men who wanted to kill you. The young man shot in the back while saving Callie was dying in your lap but now is totally healed after you crash-landed thousands miles away. You all walked away from the wreckage, and then you find out your son knows the people whose yard you have just used as a runway. Sounds like you are experiencing miracles on a regular basis, Daniel."

Everyone sat in silence as Father McDonald's words reverberated around the room. Tim peeled his back off the leather lounge, leaning towards the coffee table to pick up a plate and napkin. As quietly as possible he lifted the knife and sliced a piece of cake. The blade hit the plate as it sliced through and Tim winced at the sound. *You could hear a pin drop*, Sophia thought. She wanted to laugh at Tim with his mouth full of cake and expression of anguish. But instead, to break the silence, she said, "I'll have a piece of cake, please." Tim cut a piece and passed it to her. As she leant forward her medallion slipped out from under her shirt. With one hand, she tried to tuck it back in.

"Miracles," Tim said, between mouthfuls. "Then we really must have done something right to have been able to redeem three miracles."

"That's a lovely necklace. It looks familiar," Amy said.

"Thanks, it's a family heirloom."

"It's more than that," Jade said. Her crossed legs unwound as she pushed herself off the floor and casually stepped over the boys' splayed legs. "It's a symbol, a very powerful medallion of protection. You okay if I touch it?" Jade asked.

"Yes, but I'm not taking it off. My great-grandmother gave it to my mother to give to me. It was always handed down to the seventh daughter of the next generation of seven," Sophia said.

"Wow, seven sisters," Tim said, looking at Kath.

"Shut up, idiot."

"Kath, that's no way to speak to your brother," Sally said.

"This is serious," Kath said, "and he keeps cracking jokes."

"Just leave your brother alone."

"My great-aunt was from a family of seven girls, I think," Amy said.

Jade, still holding the twisted napkin, held out her wrist to Sophia. "My great-grandmother gave me this."

Sophia tenderly touched the bracelet and instantly felt her internal and external energy centers expanding. She withdrew her fingers, uncertain, as a stream of consciousness tried to communicate with her. Sophia said, "That's a unique bracelet."

Jade reached out and held Sophia's locket between her fingers, turning it around to see it was double-sided. The curved metal was smooth and warm from Sophia's skin. "See this," Jade said, "this symbol is Penelope's web." There was an embossed image of a ten-spoke wheel with stars at the end of each spoke. Each star had twenty sharp outward points. "This is a sign of protection. The stars are also known as the Seal of Solomon, which amplifies your locket's message of protection," she said. "The lines of the wheel and stars are interlaced by two lines joining at the center of the symbol. The symbol is composed of only two lines. It represents unity, the drawing together of people for the preservation of all. It also reflects numerological mysticism. Seventy-two: the primal magical number can be achieved with sacred geometry.

"Sophia, on the other side of your locket," Jade said, turning it over and looking at the symbol's multiple connecting spheres, "is the flower of life. It holds the secrets of the universe. It's a symbol that was created from one sphere, the first seed of life. It multiplied, spiraling out until it contained all the sacred patterns and secrets of the universe. The flower of life can be seen throughout history in religious architecture. It's in the atom, the building blocks of life. It can be found within everything: a piece of fruit, an icicle, a person or an animal. It's geometry, it's Platonic solids, it's everything."

"What are Platonic solids?" Joe asked.

"Shapes. Geometry. Like a tetrahedron — it looks like a pyramid, a hexahedron better known as a cube, and they connect with the different elements of earth like water, air, fire. All of this is within the flower of life." Jade stopped talking, looking around at the faces staring at her. She let go of the locket, smiled at Sophia apologetically then quickly looked down, nervously twisting the napkin in her hand. Her face grew redder by the second. "Anyway, that's all I know." Jade settled back next to Kevin without looking at anyone, and started to chew the ends of her long hair.

"That's all!" Tim said. "What are you, a walking Wiki? I thought K had the smarts, but you, you're good."

"Tim, don't," Kevin said.

Touched by Jade's insights, Sophia was moved and grateful for her knowledge. She herself had never thought to seek that knowledge, which now made so much sense. "Nice, Jade," Sophia said. "I've always been protected. It's a tall order, preservation of all. We might just have to go there, to the center. Where the virus began," Sophia said.

"Do we have to build an ark?" Tim asked.

Callie ignored Tim and said, "What do you mean 'the center'?"

Jade started talking at a hundred miles a minute. "The Middle East, Jerusalem, the spiritual center where it all began. It's also where the virus started, like Sophia said. We have to go back to the beginning."

Sophia sat on the floor quietly, uncrossed her legs, recrossed them lotus-style, and massaged her toes. "When we left Joe's cafe I was completely freaked; it was so surreal. The monsters we encountered can only be described as demons, stinking of garbage. It was an abomination of earthly creatures, it was beastly and they transformed back and forth into giants, and then into millions of tiny black demons. I have seen them around the heads of the infected too. I think we have been seeing the same thing."

"You're right on the money," Tim said. "We saw the same thing happening with the giants as we fled the city; they were vile. That's what chased us."

Daniel lifted up his cup and took a sip of, probably cold, tea. "You two aren't related?" he said, pointing to her and Amy.

"No," Amy said.

"Is anyone going to eat that last piece of cake?" Kath asked. She looked at Tim. "You've had three."

Amy's attention was fixed on Sophia. "What do you mean? Are you saying we have to go to Israel? That's the last place in the world you want to be right now," she said, looking at Casey. "We don't even know if anyone is still alive over there. The virus infected so many at the very beginning."

"Even if it were true, there is no way of getting there," Terry said.

Joe moved his large frame in his seat and pulled a pillow from behind his back, tucking it by his side. "I have to say, if we are supposed to walk there, we will find a road. One will open up for us. If we have to fly, then we will find a plane, and the same if we need to sail. You have to be certain it's a journey you're willing to take."

Sophia smiled at Joe, and looked deep into the energy of the room. It wasn't well lit, which highlighted each person's iridescent aura. She could feel her energy changing. Casey was looking at her strangely. Amy's book was resting in her lap and it had a soft pulsation and Sophia's vision started to blur. Everyone began to fade. Her body felt heavy, a tickle formed in her throat. Her face was itchy, crawling with hair; she felt six-feet tall and smelt of fur and ale. Stars filled her eyes. Her mouth moved and a deep, raspy male voice, distant and foreign to her ears, said from her lips: "Disease seeped through the bowels of Gehenna. You have the key now find the lock, and lay it to rest upon the golden rock, the heart of the gatekeeper, the guardian of the underworld. No end or beginning to face the heavens and the emerald heart will glow and light will be returned. The Emerald Tablet must be returned."

Sophia's throat was sore and dry and she needed water. She could feel the spirit backing away. The sensation of her face and the smallness of her head and body returned; her arms felt light. Sophia strained to open her eyes. They were glued shut. "Water, please," she said between tingling lips, happy to hear her own voice.

Casey was on his feet and soon held a glass to her mouth. "What was all that about? There was the spirit of a hooded man with a ginger beard enveloping you. I have seen him before, like when we went through the basement wall, but there was something else. What was it? I know, it was one of those canvas paintings, Amy. His portrait is in one of the old trunks in the basement."

"He could be my great, great, great-something grandfather, the owner of the book of Splendor?" Amy said.

Sophia waited for her eyes to open, and listened to the adults murmuring around her. Fresh smells of sage filled her senses, and her chest rose as she drew a breath into her belly. The familiar sound of Father McDonald praying was soothing. Everyone talked amongst themselves, eager to know what was happening.

Jade spoke up. "Trance mediumship."

"Have you seen it before?" Amy asked.

"I have seen it once, a shaman channeling the spirits of my great-grandmother's tribe. I have seen shadow dancers getting in touch with the inner wolf to tame it and I have seen coming-of-age ceremonies where the participants consumed potions to induce a trance state. But they were all controlled by a gifted elder. No offence, Sophia, but you are what, fourteen, fifteen?"

Casey hadn't moved from Sophia's side. "How are you feeling?"

Her eyes fluttered open. "Heavy, like I have been in a deep sleep."

Callie raised her voice slightly over the others. "What happened to you? Are you, or were you, in any pain?"

"No, no pain, just really weak and distant."

"Has this happened before?"

"No, nothing like this."

"Did you hear what was said?"

"Yes."

"Do you understand what it means?"

"Yes and no. Something was taken off a statue that has to be returned. Behind my eyes, I watched a slideshow of images while the man spoke."

"How do you know it was a man?" Callie asked.

"I could feel the size of his body, and I could smell his fur coat. He had a beard that made my face itch. He seemed kind, but firm and ancient."

"What were the images you saw, can you tell us?"

"I saw a picture of a statue deep underground, in a cave, I think. Over its chest was a cavity where a breastplate of armor belonged, and on it was dusty gemstone of different shapes. Then a beautiful huge old door with many locks, all closed. There was a rotten stench, a whirlpool of dark matter. It was the same as Joe's cafe. There was a sense of sand, lots of it, with thousands of people in white standing in silence holding candles as a horn was blown. The plate must be returned before the last horn blows. I think *we* have to return the breastplate. Each image was charged emotionally with either agony and anguish, or hope and joy."

"Do you have the tablet?" Kevin asked.

"No, I have no idea what or where it is." Sophia looked at Jade. "Tell me what you're thinking."

"Oh, nothing."

"Yes, you are. I can see your cogs turning," Kevin said.

"Please tell me," Sophia said.

"There is a tablet called the Emerald Tablet. It contains text that is thought to give those that possess it the ability to move between different dimensions, different worlds. It was believed to contain the knowledge from Abraham, and it was passed onto Moses and so on. Egyptian mythology puts it in the hands of Thoth. In Greek mythology, Hermes — thought to be the reincarnation of Thoth — was called 'Thrice Great' because of the three parts of his ability: the wisdom of the whole universe, alchemy, and astrology and divine influence in humanity. The mention of the Emerald Tablet pops up and appears in numerous cultures and was apparently studied by Isaac Newton, I think, who thought it to be pure ancient doctrine so he studied the scribe to understand this physical world. He believed the writings revealed secret techniques to influence the stars and the forces of nature. I'm not sure, but I think I read that his translation is housed in King's College Library, Cambridge University. But if that's the case, how can it have been removed from a statue in the Middle East. I can definitely jumble up things I have read, but —"

"Do unto others as you would have them do unto you," Father McDonald said.

"I'm lost," Tim said.

"Well," Jade told him, "basically, it means it's instrumental in maintaining the balance and structure of the universe, and the removal of it, from wherever it was, has caused the virus and an unbalance within our society. Thoth was thought to stand between good and evil. If he was, the statue that you saw, Sophia, could be his. He kept the balance between this world and the underworld and had the power to heal."

Sophia witnessed Jade's aura pulse with excitement. Everyone else seemed confused.

"Also, I have been thinking about an equation: $S = k \log W$."

"What does it mean?" Sophia asked.

"Entropy," Jade said.

"Speak English, people. We're not all intels," Tim said. "My head's hurting."

"Entropy," Callie interrupted, "is a measurement of disorder or randomness. Order to disorder. Move from an ordered state to disordered states. Life is filled with entropy." Callie took a breath.

And Jade jumped in. "Making order from chaos; it's exhilarating. Entropy is a measure of molecular randomness, or disorder. The second law of thermodynamics, any spontaneous process increases the disorder of the universe and —"

"There she goes again," Tim said, rolling his eyes.

"Sorry, it's just stimulating," Jade said and stopped talking.

"Never apologize for who you are, Jade. It is exciting. Where are you going with this?" Kevin said.

Sophia saw Jade physically start to fatigue. Her brain had used up so much energy, she needed more. Sophia nudged Casey and whispered, "Give her a zap, she's exhausted."

Casey, wide-eyed, said, "No, I'll hurt her."

"No, you won't," she whispered back. "I promise."

Casey looked into Jade's ethereal body and rubbed his hands together. He clapped and coughed, thinking it would somehow disguise his intentions.

"What the hell are you clapping at?" Tim said. "You scared the shit out me. You've got a sonic boom for a clap, mate."

Kevin cracked up, Casey smiled and Sophia had to turn her head, to disguise her laughter. Jade stretched and her aura expanded, rippling into Tim's, giving him a static shock.

"What is the reactive state?" Jade continued with a surge of energy. "It is a state of being. A person's actions or thoughts without pause. A negative thought while in a negative state can trigger natural disasters – like when someone gossips or is jealous – a reactive state is a negative state of being that creates a reaction upon the collective human soul and the planet. We can change a negative effect into a positive state — sort of like the butterfly effect — we have a negative right now, so how do we change that negative to a positive one? By being proactive and actively changing the effect; that is, by reversing the negative action or creating order from the disorder. This doesn't make any sense to you, does it?"

Callie continued, so Jade could catch her breath and slow down. "Yes, it does. But you can't eliminate chaos. The Big Bang is the most ordered state and entropy was at its lowest. We can't go back to the seed. You can't reverse a butterfly flapping its wings."

Jade jumped back in again. "Well, why not? We can go back to the chain of events that started this current mess and create a better outcome for humanity. Or at least put back what was removed, making the statue whole again — order from chaos. K may be able to create windows in time," Jade said.

"K, enlighten me, buddy. What are they talking about?" Tim said.

"Return the missing artefact that unleashed hell. Change undesirable to a desirable," Kevin said.

"I'm tired," Tim said.

"I'm sorry, you're losing me too. Windows in time?" Father McDonald said.

"The way I see it," Joe said, "is that we have lots of chaos and we can choose how we will shuffle the broken pieces to create balance and harmony. Forgetting science for a moment, we need to bring back the smile on people's faces, the love in their eyes, the gentle touch of the wind and to see the crystal colors of the light. As Sophia said, we need to have certainty." Joe looked up to the ceiling and said, "We beseech you, God, with the power of your greatness help us undo this entanglement."

"Amen," said Father McDonald.

"I'm way too tired to keep this conversation going," said Terry. "How about we get some sleep and maybe we will find some answers in the morning."

"That sounds like a good idea," Amy said.

"Jade," Sophia said as everyone started to move, "you're right, we have to make a change. Your thinking has been the reason why you're here. You have been searching in your mind for a way to find your mother and she has a burning desire to heal the world of this virus."

"Thanks, Sophia," Jade said. The floodgates opened and Jade's eyes were shiny with tears, but she didn't let a drop spill.

Sophia tasted a change in the air and sat down on the edge of the lounge. She screwed up her nose in concentration and watched everyone stretch and yawn, agreeing it was time for bed. Joe was already on his feet helping Father McDonald, and Tim was telling Kevin his head hurt from all the thinking. Sophia stood up next to Casey. Suddenly the lights began to flicker, pulsating. She looked at Casey and he wanted to take her hand.

"It's not me," he said.

They were all drawn together, reducing the space between them and found themselves standing still in the middle of the room. Amy still had hold of her book and it became illuminated. Sophia saw Kevin's head turn towards Amy. *He must be sensing it too*, she thought. Sophia's necklace, hidden by the depth of radiance from Amy's book, now surged with light. She hadn't noticed it ever come alive before. It felt buzzy, effervescent, against her skin. The room became animated, filled with whispers and fogged images.

Father McDonald said in a soft voice, "The dead. The fragile curtain between the living and the dead is dissolving."

The power in the room intensified. Shadowy phantoms appeared. The energy of the ghostly forms was compressing, and they almost looked solid, physically alive, although with the absence of consciousness. No different from the infected, the only difference being that these bodies were long dead. Nobody spoke and Sophia felt confused, vulnerable and alarmed, almost stunned by the apparitions. The distance and aloofness she had felt in her visions had turned into foreboding; she felt mortal amongst the ghosts and became aware of her love of life. *The smell of a flower, the touch of the wind, sun on her face, and laughter — they are heaven,* she thought and looped her pinkie with Casey's. Slowly, the energy dropped and the phantoms and shadows faded and so, too, the circle of light that united and protected them vanished. *The world is dying, becoming the promised living hell. Since the removal of the Emerald Tablet the veil has been lifted and the dead must be rising.*

"This is the third time this has happened," Casey said, "and it's getting stronger."

"Are we safe?" Sally asked. "Why has God forsaken us?"

Father McDonald took Sally's hands in his. "He hasn't forsaken us, Sally. He brought us together to help one another."

"We will be safe," Sophia said. "There is an angel watching over us, battling on a higher realm for our victory. Down here, this is our battle to overcome."

Terry yawned, rubbed his eyes and put his arm around Amy's shoulders. "Let's get a few hours' sleep and talk about this in the morning."

Callie hugged Kevin, Tim and Jade. "Look after each other," she said.

"I can't go to sleep after that!" Tim protested as Callie let him go.

Kevin headed up the stairs with Jade and Tim, watching his mom and dad walk across the foyer to their room saying their good nights. The door closed quietly behind them. Sophia heard the faintest click as Joe helped Father McDonald wearily up the stairs.

THE GHOSTS HAD TRIED to touch him. He was burning up so much his shirt clung to his body. Shaun lay still on the bottom bunk listening to squeaky old stairs as everyone ascended to their rooms. He rolled over on his side, facing away from the bedroom door and listened to Kevin, Casey and Tim enter the room. Without turning on the light, they changed, ready for bed. Shaun was glad he was no longer alone. Casey was talking about caves, green armor and flying creatures. Shaun was feeling shaky, anxious. Their jabbering about caves and statues frustrated him. His stomach tightened, aching. "Will you assholes shut up?" he said, with clenched teeth. The sound in the room was reduced to whispers and shuffling, and ruffling of sheets as they climbed into bed. Shaun searched his mind for something to focus on and the image he conjured was a good day at the beach with his parents. They had built a sandcastle and they were creating a moat and tunnels around it.

His eyes darted back and forth as he drifted into sleep and dreams of falling into one of the tunnels around the sandcastle, and the sand starting to collapse around him. The ocean was rising and streaming into the moat; he ran, looking for a way in and found an entrance under the castle. He climbed some stairs and reached the top expecting to see the ocean and his parents, but he saw a barren landscape with mountains of sand in the dead of night. One single light was shining in the distance. He looked back down the stairs and could see the frothy ocean water rising up. He couldn't go back, only forward. He walked across the sand towards the light and it never seemed to get any closer. It was moving from side to side. It was a lantern, held by somebody, guiding him. It appeared to take hours, but the sun didn't rise. There was movement under the sand and occasionally, if he stopped moving forward, he started to sink. *Where am I? It feels familiar.*

He was getting excited as he continued to approach the light and he felt the warmth of the sun on his back, but there was no sun or moon in the sky. A shapely woman stood behind the lantern calling out his name and he wanted to run towards her. Tears were trapped in his throat, hope teased his heart. She called out his name, urging him to hurry. Shaun ran. His legs were getting heavy and he lifted each leg higher and higher. The sand was wet, the foaming water of the ocean had followed him to this place. It was getting harder to move; he was sinking in the wet sand. She called out to him again. "Hurry, we have to go back." He was immobilized in the sand — it had become thick like ice, holding him around the waist. He knew that voice, laced with the maturity of a woman and the pleading of a child. He could hear the beauty of her soul, the rhythm of each word touched his heart. It was Rachel. As soon as he said her name, there was an explosion of light behind her. He sank down into the sand, struggling to be free as it buried him alive.

The smell of freshly cooked food aroused his olfactory

senses and his body was filled with sounds. His shoulders were pressed into the mattress and he heard giggling. It was Alex. Tim told Alex it was okay to go ahead and body-slam Shaun, and Casey said it wasn't okay because he was dreaming. How did Casey know he was dreaming? A cold little finger touched his eye, lifting up his eyelid. Shaun lunged at his neck playfully like a rabid dog going for the kill. Alex squealed and fell to the floor. Shaun watched Alex's face turn into a smile then a serious knot appeared on his tiny brow.

"Are you crying? Are you sad?" Alex asked. He pushed himself up off the carpet.

Tim hung his head over the side of the bunk.

"No, buddy, I'm not crying," Shaun said, reaching out to slap Tim's head and caught a handful of hair. He pushed Tim's face away.

"Breakfast is ready," Alex said. "Mommy said I could wake you."

Shaun pulled up the sheet and wiped his face quickly before tossing them back and stepping into his jeans.

"Morning," Casey said.

"Morning," Shaun grumbled. He kept his head low, avoiding eye contact. He collected the clean blue t-shirt Terry had given him and said to Alex, "Lead the way, dude." He pulled the shirt over his head, walking out the door.

Shaun and Alex went past the bathroom. Shaun stepped back, feeling the urge to go to the toilet. Alex continued to follow him into the bathroom. "No, buddy, you wait here." Shaun closed the door and Alex slid down the wall and squatted against it, waiting.

Shaun leant on the washbasin, looking at his reflection in the mirror. He splashed water over his eyes and cheeks, washing away traces of tears. The cool water felt refreshing in his hands and on his face. He was quite sticky from the night and couldn't resist having a shower. He let the water cascade over his head, trying to erase the images from the dream. There was a knock and Alex's muffled voice asking him how much longer he was going to be, because he was alone and scared in the dark hall. Shaun turned off the water, quickly toweled himself dry and dressed. He left the room feeling lighter and maybe even a little invigorated.

"Now are you ready?" Alex asked as the bathroom light flooded into the hallway. Alex pushed against the wall and stood up.

The odd pair walked along the short corridor to the stairs. Shaun's foot was poised ready to step down, but he stopped, and looked back towards the bedroom and down to the end of the hall. The boards covering the end window made the corridor appear dark and mistrusting, creating a creepy feeling. Shaun had a sense of being watched.

5

MELTING POT: ENGLAND

Daniel reached for the tea towel to help Terry dry the dishes after lunch. Joe was already cooking a stew for dinner. "That smells great, Joe."

Shaun came in through the back door. "There's a motorcycle in the barn. Can I take Alex for a ride?"

Terry looked at Daniel and shrugged his shoulders. "It's up to you. They're your boys."

Daniel was going to correct him, but then turned to Shaun. "Have you ever ridden a motorcycle before?"

"Sure, heaps of times. My mate had a dirt bike and we used to churn up the school grounds."

"You did what?" Terry said. "You can't take it out if you're going to wreak havoc around the place."

"No, that's not what I meant. I just meant I know how to handle a motorcycle."

Daniel looked at Shaun and said nothing.

"I won't let anything happen to him, I promise," Shaun said.

"How many promises have you made in your life? Ten, twenty, a hundred?" Daniel asked.

"Two," Shaun said.

Daniel shifted his weight to his right leg and put a dry plate into the overhead cupboard. "I think I'll go take a look. I have my own motorcycle back home," Daniel said to Terry. He draped the tea towel on the edge of the bench to dry.

"The keys are on the hook over there by the door."

Daniel unhooked the keys. "Come on then, let's have some fun." Daniel and Shaun walked over to the shed together to find Alex sitting stretched out on the seat. He was trying to reach the handlebars pretending he was speeding down a racetrack.

Daniel lifted Alex off, and wheeled the bike outside. He climbed on, started the bike, and kicked up the stand. "Get on," he said to Shaun.

Shaun hesitated.

"Get on."

Shaun threw his leg over and hung onto the back of the bike. Daniel put it into gear and took off. They cruised on the Bonnie down the driveway, past the plane wreckage, and turned around heading towards the hedges at the back of the house. They slid a little on the wet grass and Daniel stretched his leg forward for balance. The other kids watched them until they were out of sight.

Alex was jumping up and down on the spot waiting for his turn. Daniel stopped in front of Alex. Daniel swapped with Shaun, jumping on the back. Once Daniel felt Shaun was confident with a pillion passenger, he tapped him on the shoulder and pointed to Alex. Shaun turned the motorcycle and headed for the kid. Daniel jumped off and put Alex on the back. "Now you hold on to Shaun tight with your arms, and squeeze his hips with your legs, okay? Shaun, don't go above second gear, alright?"

Shaun slowly let out the clutch and accelerated. He

stayed in first gear down to the fence and did a wide U-turn at the bottom of the driveway. He did this about four times to Alex's delight. The other kids were perched on a log looking out into the silver birch trees.

Tim got up and walked over to Daniel. "Can I have a turn?"

"No, mate."

"Why not? You let Shaun ride it."

"He's a little older than you. When you're his age you can ride it."

"He's not that much older."

"He's old enough to have a license. You're not. Don't argue, you cheeky monkey." Daniel ruffled his hair. "You can get on the back."

"No, I'm good."

Shaun was coming back up the driveway and Daniel walked over towards him. Shaun stopped. "Listen, the others aren't allowed to ride it on their own. You can take them for a ride on the back. The sky is really overcast. I don't suppose the rain will stay away for too long. When you're done, put it back in the shed and put the key where it belongs, okay?"

"Sure, no sweat, will do."

Kevin, Casey, Jade and Sophia were walking towards Tim. They stopped and watched Shaun and Alex for a minute before heading to the house as if they were carrying the weight of the world on their shoulders.

"Where are you guys headed?" Daniel asked Kevin.

"Inside. It looks terrible out here, and the air feels strange," he said.

"Is Father McDonald alright over there?" he asked Sophia.

"Yes, he will pray until he feels the evil is pushed back."

Daniel looked out over to Father McDonald sitting on the ground on his knees, unwavering. "He hasn't slept much. He looks a little pale."

"He never does. He is always pale these days. It's his heart, it's physically weak but he pretends it's okay. He doesn't want me to know."

Daniel held the door open for them to pass, taking a glimpse over his shoulder at his son and Shaun. He could hear Alex shouting, "Slow, slow, slow." And Shaun went very slow. Then Alex yelled, "Faster, faster, faster." And Shaun would speed up. They were having a ball of a time just going up and down the driveway. Kevin was exceptional with amazing gifts, but so was Alex. He had the biggest heart that melted the toughest characters.

ON THE RUG by the bookshelves Shaun handed Alex the gemstones from his pouch. He focused on listening, watching Amy and Father McDonald out of the corner of his eye, while teaching Alex a game. Amy closed her book gently in her lap and moved out of the high-backed leather chair under the stained-glass lamp, which bathed the lounge room with a soft glow of color. She offered her seat to Father McDonald. "Come and make yourself comfortable," she said. "This chair is extremely comfortable."

"What are you reading?" Father McDonald asked, nodding towards her book. "It's a book of light. It's filled with the mysteries of the universe." She handed the book to him and he accepted. It felt light even though it was as thick as an old encyclopedia. He opened the book, surprised it was in Aramaic. "Can you read this?" he said, looking at Amy excitedly.

"Unfortunately, no, I can't. The letters, they look like symbols to me, and I remember when I was a child I would watch my grandfather run his finger under the letters as if reading from right to left and then turn the pages in the same direction. I scan over the pages and don't comprehend a single sentence. It was passed down through the generations to my grandfather and I feel him and I feel closer to God every time I open the book. I was always intrigued and would watch his face reflecting the light from the book in his hands."

"If you can't read the words, how do you know it holds the mysteries of the universe?"

"I just do," and with that said, she placed the book on the side table under the glow of the lamp, and a rainbow of colors shone across its cover.

"It's bedtime, Alex," Callie called from the other room.

Amy walked past Shaun and Alex, and as she did Shaun scooped up the gems to play another game with Alex.

She tapped on Callie's door. "You have beautiful children," she said, standing at the threshold. "Molly is a gorgeous happy little girl."

"Do you plan to have any more children?" Callie asked, stepping from the room.

"We want a big family. My great-aunt was from a large family of girls, who spread out across the world, eventually losing contact with one another. My great-aunt was my only surviving relative, although we didn't know of her until she had passed away. This was her place, which she left to me."

"That's sad," Callie said.

"What happened to Casey that day?" Amy asked.

"What do you mean?"

"Kevin said he was there, that he saw Casey. At first we believed him when he came home crying, swearing he saw a boy drown in the river, so we called the police. They were searching for days but there was nothing. They started to say Kevin had made it up. We too thought he was seeking attention. I had been overseas and soon after I got back my parents were killed in a car accident. He had told me to tell them not to come, but it was too late, they were already on their way."

"Oh, I'm sorry to hear that."

"He was very close to them. He blames himself and thinks I blame him too."

Molly was sucking on her bottle, drifting off to sleep in Callie's arms.

"May I?" Amy said, reaching out for Molly.

Callie carefully passed Molly over and Amy walked back into the living room and sat down.

"You look as if you're a natural," Callie said, following her.

"I hope so. I'm about four months," Amy said.

She's pregnant, Shaun thought. Why would she let us stay knowing she is pregnant? Wouldn't she want to protect her unborn baby?

"How exciting. Congratulations!" Callie said.

"It's ironic how in times of such despair life continues. If we listen to Casey, I'm having twins."

"What do you mean, if you listen to Casey?"

"He sometimes senses the future."

Shaun was intrigued and tried to move closer without Alex noticing.

"Really? Kevin's a bit like that." Callie turned towards the door and Amy followed her gaze. There was no one there. The boys came down the stairs and into the room seconds after her stare.

"I can see where he gets it from," Amy said.

"What me? No, I don't think so." Amy sat back, ignoring her numb arm from the impossible weight of someone so tiny, and watched Molly sleep.

The boys walked past Shaun and Alex. Kevin stopped, curious. "What are they?"

Shaun didn't answer, but scooped up the stones, tucking them into his pouch. Casey, Tim and Kevin continued into the kitchen.

"Shaun, why don't you go with Kevin? Alex, it's time for bed."

"Oh Mom, no, one more game."

"I'm sorry, Alex, it's way past your bedtime, and besides Shaun has played with you all day."

"Can I fall asleep with Molly and Amy, on the lounge? And you put me to bed later?"

Amy watched Tim and Kevin come out of the kitchen with snacks for the rest of the gang upstairs in Casey's room. Kevin tossed a packet of crisps to Shaun and handed him a coke.

"Come on," Casey said.

Shaun reluctantly got up and followed the boys upstairs.

CASEY TOOK the old stairs two at a time, trying to figure out what he could say to Shaun to help him be more trusting and open up. Casey could feel things were going to get worse. Shaun tripped on the carpet at the top of the stairs. Tim laughed and Casey reached out for Shaun's arm. Casey felt like he had been tasered and stabbed in the heart all at once; life and joy vanished, leaving feelings of guilt and abandonment. Casey felt emotionally bankrupt and suddenly alone. The image of Shaun lying across his mother's chest, crying so hard he had to be forcefully removed from the sterile room by a man Casey assumed was his father. Shaun shook off Casey's hold and the scene in his mind faded. Casey became aware of his own emotions and felt vulnerable. The images had aroused a sense of loss.

"What the hell are you staring at?" Shaun snapped.

"Your mom died when you were a kid. It wasn't your fault. You're carrying a shitload of guilt. Let it go, you're not the cause of her illness."

"Who told you that? Who told you about my mom? One of your stupid new friends?"

Tim had been laughing at Shaun when he tripped; Casey saw he was straight-faced now, with a look of caution. He walked into the bedroom, leaving Casey and Shaun alone in the dark hallway.

"You told me, just then, when I helped you up. I pick up shit and you've got a truckload."

"You're weird."

"I lost my mom last year. She was crushed during a freak tornado. I didn't get a chance to say goodbye, but you did and you should cherish that."

"Who are you to tell me what I should do?"

"There was nothing more important to her than you," Casey said to him. "She saw the gift you had brought for her." Casey looked down at the ground, then up to the ceiling, then stared at Shaun's face searching for a connection. "You took something extremely valuable, priceless."

Shaun instinctively touched his pocket. "I don't know what you're talking about," he said. He walked into the bedroom, chucked the packet of chips at Tim and threw himself onto the bed. Casey watched him: *You know exactly what I was talking about*.

"I love this room," said Sophia. "I thought my room at the convent was special because I had a window. This, this is such a beautiful blue. It's endless, like the sky, and the bunk beds built into the wall with the archways is just magical. The lower beds are practically the size of a double bed. Look at these little nooks for bookshelves cut out of the bedheads. And a little portal that must look onto the lawn. If it wasn't covered up I'm sure it would look lovely. This is a beautiful home, Casey. I would pick this for my bedroom and all my friends could come for a slumber party." Sophia's shoulders drooped and the enthusiasm trickled away as she remembered her friends Gemma and Lisa lying face down in the car park with blood pooling around them.

"Give it a rest. What century are you from? And did you say you live in a convent?" Shaun said, lying on his bed flicking his shoes off. They just missed hitting her.

"Pretty much," Sophia said, sitting on the edge of his bed.

Casey watched her effervescent aura change to darker tones. "This wasn't the original design, of course. The real estate agent said Amy's great-aunt redesigned it as a B&B. That's why there are four beds and a sitting area in this room," Casey said.

"It looks like a studio. The layout is a great use of the space," Jade said, sitting at the writing desk nestled amongst more bookshelves.

"If you girls talk about the curtains," Tim said, "I'm going to puke."

"Where's Kath?" Sophia asked.

"She won't hang with us. We're too immature for her," Tim said.

"I think you spoke too soon," Kevin said.

"What?" Tim said.

"Wait for it, " said Sophia. There was a gentle knock on the door and Kath walked in and everyone laughed.

"What's the joke?" Kath asked, looking down at her clothes.

Kevin, Casey and Sophia looked at each other with understanding.

Jade and Tim looked at them as if they had lost their minds.

"It's nothing," Jade said. "Synchronicity I presume. Your timing is impeccable. They were just wondering why you weren't here."

Kath walked across the room and plunked herself down onto the two-seater. She stretched her legs out towards the beds and with her back to Jade snatched the packet of open chips off the table and took a handful.

Sophia watched her munch on the chips, trying to get Shaun's attention. *She was going about it the wrong way. But then what do I know about boys?* Sophia thought.

"How're your hands, Shaun?" Jade asked.

"Why? They're fine, you know that," Shaun said.

"Look, we need to cut the crap and get down to why we were all brought here. I don't know about you guys, but I want to go home," Jade said.

She's right, Sophia thought. No more procrastination, it was time. Sophia climbed up on the bed above Shaun.

"Sophia," Jade said, "there are things you said last night, the message. *We have the key, now find the lock.* We know the lock is the Emerald Tablet."

Sophia and Casey's intuition heightened. Shaun sat himself up on the bed and leant against the boarded window.

"The second thing was, we need to get to a cave somewhere in the Middle East, and the third —"

She was interrupted by Shaun. "What the hell are you on about? For an intel, you are thick. Who told you? How do you know?"

"Know what?" Jade said.

"He wasn't with us last night, he'll have no idea what we're talking about," Kevin said.

Shaun's aura expanded and he was covered in reds and oranges. He wanted to know what was going on, but he was angry.

"Sophia believes — we all believe—" Casey said, looking around at everyone in the room, "we have survived and united to right a wrong that has caused the world to go haywire and the virus to magnify."

Shaun blurted out, "What makes you guys so unique? We are all going to die anyway. The world is getting smaller and smaller if you haven't noticed. We are all stuck in one house."

"You should believe more than anyone!" Jade said. "The flesh was falling off your burnt hands, you were shot in the back. What more do you need to see that you are a vital cog in a bigger picture? Like I was saying, we need to place the Emerald Tablet back where it came from, but we don't know where that is."

Kevin interjected. "What about the rest of the message? That was just the first line."

"We'll have to work it out as we go," Casey said.

"That's it in a nutshell," Tim said. "I know how we can get there!"

Sophia looked at Tim and saw Kevin was becoming restless and nearly jumped off the bed when Jade shouted out, "Of course! Kevin!"

"That was my moment," Tim said, throwing up his hands and smacking them down into his lap spilling his chips in frustration.

"Whatever," Jade said, raising her eyebrows. "He can take us anywhere in the world."

"I can't," Kevin said. "I have never been to the Middle East. I wouldn't know how to begin."

"Just like the plane crash. We passed through some window in time that Kevin opened. Do you know how we met? He found me lying on the forest floor about to be mauled by a wolf. Where? On the south coast of the United States! We escaped into something similar to a plasma energy field that shimmered and sparkled like a mirage. When we stepped through, it was magnificent. We emerged a few hours later. Where, you ask? Get this — on the other side of the world in Australia. It was so intense. When we arrived at his home, what seemed like a typical day to Kevin and Tim was actually three days later. The cops were looking for them." Jade had her hands on her hips for emphasis.

"I saw those cops from my roof," Shaun said, "and I saw Kevin and Tim on their bikes in the bush vanish into thin air. I waited for hours. I even fell asleep and that was two days before the cops started casing the streets."

"You were watching us?" Tim said.

"Get over yourself," Shaun said and threw the pillow at him.

"Anyway," Jade said, feasting her eyes on Sophia, "when we were being chased, he opened a portal that was paper-thin and we practically landed on his grandmother's porch within seconds and we had been miles away. The adults still seemed to be clueless. It must be their defense mechanism."

"Kilometers," Tim corrected.

"And that's how we got here. When the plane was going down he opened a doorway. He can get us there, even if he thinks he doesn't know how."

"The image," Kevin said, rubbing the back of his head, "needs to be emotionally charged. The picture of Casey and Sophia riding the motorbike was emotionally charged. We have to focus on the message."

Casey, his cheeks on fire, said, "What about a demo?"

"Yeah, retard, give us a demo. Idiots."

"Why are you being so mean?" Kath asked.

"Mean? You should have seen what your golden boyfriend did to some dumb fuck on the train," Shaun said.

"What?" Kath said.

"I saw him across the road from our place smashing up the neighbor's car. He's infected," Tim said. "Sorry, Kath."

"Can we get back on topic?" Jade said.

"Who died and made you queen?" Shaun said to Jade.

"Why are we so agitated all of a sudden?" Casey asked.

"Enough, guys!" Kevin said. "If I open up a doorway, I don't know how to calculate the time. Our parents will freak if we disappear on them again."

"I was thinking about that," Jade said. "Kath, you stated that they were gone for three days, and the boys thought it was only a day. That would break down to ..."

Sophia saw Jade's mind ticking over. "We need to keep continuity, and not over-complicate things with facts," Sophia said.

"I'm not doing it," Kevin said.

"Go on, K. Show them what you can do. What about just from one room to another?" Tim said.

"That's a good idea, Tim," Jade said.

"Thanks."

"I don't know."

"Come on, creep, show us how you do it," Shaun said.

"Don't call me that."

"Why? What are you going to do?"

"Nothing, it just makes you look stupid, that's all. It doesn't bother me."

Sophia watched Kevin take in a deep breath, rub his hands on his knees and walk towards the center of the room.

"Okay, off the beds and come stand behind me." They did as he said. Except for Shaun.

"You missed some," Sophia said, pointing to Tim's shirt. Tim looked down and finished picking off the chip crumbs before brushing himself down. He made her smile; he wasn't bothered about what others thought. Tim was true to himself.

"Wait," shouted Shaun. "You got a knife?" he asked Casey.

"Sure, a pocket knife. Why?"

"Can I have it?"

Casey opened the desk door and fished out the knife and gave it to Shaun. He flicked it open and sliced into his own leg. Blood started to soak into his jeans. He hobbled in behind Kevin.

"What did you do that for?" Tim asked.

"He wants to see if it heals. Isn't that right?" Jade said, watching him wipe the blade clean on his other leg and place the knife in his pocket.

"You're not just a pretty face, are you?"

"Okay, K," Tim said. "Let's go."

"Relax as much as you can," Jade said softly. Sophia waited beside Casey and Tim. Kevin's hands rested by his side. His pinkie reached out, finding Jade, and she responded. Their auras began to pulse with light. She watched as a fluid spiral of energy came from Kevin's fore-head, chest and abdomen, joining into one swirl and the molecules in space retracted, opening a shimmering water-fall of light in front of them. He let go of Jade's finger, stepped forward, merged into the light and disappeared.

"Doesn't it look like embryonic fluid?" Jade said, moving up and touching it with her hand. Light rippled across its surface as if it was alive and sensitive to her touch.

"It looks like thin jelly to me," Tim said, "and it feels just as cool and smooth." He stepped away from Sophia and Casey. Arms elevated at chest height, like a zombie, he walked straight through.

Casey and Shaun, a little more cautiously, followed. "You're not coming, Kath?" Sophia asked.

"No, thanks, I'll wait right here and hold down the fort."

Sophia stepped through feeling alive and at peace. Every moment that was, is, or will be, seemed to be one moment in time. She felt like the seed. The freshness was cleansing. *What an amazing world*, she thought, *it is so blissful.* Someone touched her hand and tugged and she fell onto the cold tiles. Sophia looked up and saw Shaun sitting on the toilet. Tim looked like he was waiting for a bus, and Jade was sucking on the ends of her hair blocking the bathroom door. Casey was down on one knee peering into her face. Kevin was standing over her. "You have to stay focused and keep moving through," Kevin said to her.

"Why? What will happen?" she asked.

"I don't know, but we were all in this room within seconds of each other," he said. "Except you."

Jade pushed off the door and said, "You, awesomely, have been gone for twenty-two minutes."

"But it only seemed like a few," Sophia said, getting up from the cold tiles.

"Exactly!"

They piled out of the bathroom and into the bedroom.

Kath was pacing the floor. "What the hell happened to just popping into the next room and back?" she said, looking at Tim and Kevin.

"We had to wait for Sophia. She was — she got — stuck," Tim said, bouncing onto the bed. Sophia sat next to him and he quickly jumped off.

Energized, Jade plonked herself down onto the bed next to Sophia, and Casey joined them. Tim and Kevin sat on the floor and swung their legs up onto the side of the bed.

Shaun walked in and Kath ran to check his leg. It was healed.

Shaun couldn't believe what had just happened. His dad was right, but how could Kevin open a doorway without the artefact.

"How is your leg?" Kath asked.

He lifted himself up onto the edge of the bay window. "Not a scratch," he said, sticking his finger in the hole of the pants. He rested his chin on his knees and wished he could see out the window.

"How do we find the tablet?" Kevin asked.

"It has to be in the Middle East somewhere. It's the center," Sophia said.

"Kevin's got it," Shaun said.

"What?" Kevin said, sitting up and pushing his hair out of his eye. "Are you mad? Why would you say that?"

Shaun kept quiet, not sure how far to go. It was agony. He wanted to tell them, he wanted to trust them. He looked at Casey and felt vulnerable, then figured what the hell.

"I know what it can do. I've seen it and what you just did. You need the breastplate of Thoth. The tablet, you've got to know where it is."

"I swear I don't have it. I don't know how I can do what I do. I swear, I never heard of it until the other day."

"What? How do you know?" Jade said, amazed.

"My dad was an archaeologist and he was part of a dig in the desert in Israel. I was only young, seven years old. It was rumored that they found a cave with lost artefacts and a statue of an Egyptian god. He possessed the key to other worlds, and the cure for all ailments."

"Who is the intel now?" Jade said, trying to lighten the mood.

"But how do you know all this?" Casey asked.

"I was there. My mother was in hospital and she begged my dad to take me. He left me outside the cave for hours with the head archaeologist's daughter, Rachel. We were both young and frightened. They found the tablet and my father destroyed everyone who could finger him, including Rachel. He got me to shove the tablet into the bottom of the suitcase; it was green, extremely heavy. We boarded a plane. He drugged me soon after so I am only starting to remember bits and pieces. We delivered it to some Russian oil tycoon in Egypt who promised my dad he would pay him millions, and allow him to use it the once to heal my mother. He received the money and flew back for her. It was a week before she was able to fly. Egyptian Customs denied us entrance. My father told them we were expected. They took him away and brought him back bruised and bloody. They allowed him to clean himself up, then put us on the next flight out. My mother died soon after."

Everyone was quiet. The boys still lay on the floor, looking everywhere but at Shaun, except Casey who was resting his head in his hands and turned towards Sophia, then Shaun, and smiled.

"Do you know who the Russian was, and where he took it?" Sophia asked.

"No, all I remember is seeing Egyptian passports — I was lying on a red and gold couch and a woman put a pillow under my head — then hearing an argument and the promise. There was a little boy playing on the ground, making sounds of airplanes and gunfire. The next I remember we were landing in Australia and I was throwing up. I vowed never to trust my dad again."

Kevin sat next to him on the bed and said, "Well, that's why you're here. To help right your dad's wrong and return the artefact."

"Rachel and I saw those tiny winged demons, the ones now saturating the atmosphere, fight each other to get out of the cave. That was ten years ago. If you guys think they were the virus, the beginning, why didn't I get sick back then?"

6

THE SHE-DEVIL: ENGLAND

Kevin, upstairs in Casey's bedroom, felt a roller coaster of emotions emanating from downstairs — and it wasn't a barrel of laughs. His mom was becoming aware of him, so he pulled back. But something wasn't right and he felt long dirty nails drag down his face to his stomach. His internal alarm screamed.

Next to him lying on the floor, legs perched over the edge of the bed, were Tim and Casey. *When did the room go quiet? When did they stop talking?* he wondered. It was like the day before his nanna and pop died. Bile suddenly rose in his throat, the color draining from his cheeks. His eyes focused on Shaun nestled in the window frame, squeezing his leather pouch. Something was wrong.

"Something's wrong downstairs. I don't feel good," Kevin said and swung his legs off the bed and sat up.

"What's wrong?" Jade asked.

Kevin stood up listening, the silence distressing. Casey also stood, straining to see beyond the shadows. Kevin went for the door, Tim and Casey on his heels. They stormed down the hallway towards the front of the house and slid down the banister.

Kevin jumped clear and heaved opened the massive double doors to the lounge room. The light of the log fire danced hypnotically, casting a field of shadows across the adult faces, and the chill crept into the room.

Molly and Alex were asleep on the lounge. Simultaneously, they started making noises in their sleep. Alex was the first to let out a little giggle and then Molly.

Callie looked at Kevin. "Why the dramatic entrance?" She tried to see his eyes. "What's wrong?"

Casey ran into the room, stopping beside Kevin, and froze. He could see the fiery red vapors of a she-devil. Her long, poisonous yellow nails were trailing down Alex's sleeping face. Three menacing phantom spirits, her entourage, toyed with Molly, and looked back at the she-devil like dogs on a leash seeking approval.

"Casey, Kevin, you're scaring us," Amy said.

"Wake them up," Casey said.

"What do you see?" Kevin asked, his voice full of anguish. "I can feel it, but I can't see it."

Casey didn't have time to explain. He shot out a bolt of energy at the phantoms around Molly.

Tim's mom, whispering, said, "Shh, there's no harm. They could be having a beautiful dream of sliding down rainbows, just like those care bears you guys used to love."

"Wake them up!" Casey said. "You have to wake them up now!"

Callie stood up and went to Alex. "Kevin, what's going on?"

"I'm not sure, but you have to listen to him. There's something terrible happening."

Amy was sitting close to Molly, when her little face suddenly turned red and she was holding her breath. Amy quickly picked Molly up, turned her over and hit her on the back. Amy stopped and placed her hand on Molly's little back and smiled. "I can feel her little heartbeat." Molly gasped for air, coughed and screamed, as if in extreme pain. Her milk and dinner gushed from her mouth all over Amy. Her rosy cheeks were changing back to normal as she continued to wail.

Daniel took Molly and kissed her face. She was burning up. "Thank you," he said to Amy. He held his baby girl to his chest, blowing air on her head, and her crying turned into hiccoughs and sobs.

Casey could see the spirits concentrating on Alex as Father McDonald crouched on the floor praying loudly and flicking the pages of his Bible. "First they play with them, making them laugh, next they take their souls," Father McDonald said.

"Who are they?" Daniel asked. "I am so over this shit." He patted Molly and gently bounced her, trying to soothe her.

Watching his mom trying to waken Alex was agonizing. Kevin clapped and yelled, "Alex, buddy, wake up!"

Molly's crying and Alex's giggling mixed together was haunting. *What can I do? What can I do?* Casey searched his mind for answers when Shaun walked into the room and stood beside him.

"What's happening?"

Casey didn't answer. He was fixed on the evil spirits, pushing them with his energy, away from Molly and Daniel. They backed off and moved slightly, guarding the she-devil.

"Come on, little man," Kevin said to his brother, "or it's body-slam time for you."

Shaun walked straight to Alex and held onto his foot as if trying to keep him in this world and said, "Why won't he wake up? Alex, one more game. Wake up, Alex, we can play one more game! Come on, Alex, you're my pal."

Alex was laughing like he was being tickled to death, before he went quiet, his body went limp, and he collapsed in Callie's arms.

Everything was happening too fast. Casey expanded his energy force, driving the she-devil's entourage aside and began covering Alex with a shield of energy. He pushed and pushed, focusing streams of energy into the spirit world; his head pounded, his nose started to bleed. He wasn't powerful enough. His energy was like a punch underwater and merely stunned the she-devil. It turned its evil eyes to him and hissed, its mouth dropping open to its chest. It expelled a high-pitched shriek that vibrated through everything and everyone. The room shook like an earthquake. Its tentacles of energy, a hundred times more powerful, swatted Casey across the room. He slammed hard against the wall. His chest felt crushed, he couldn't breathe.

Sophia stumbled into the room holding her ears, protecting herself from the sound of the she-devil's high-pitched scream. Casey's skin crawled. Sophia could see and feel what he saw, and the malevolent spirit saw her too. It hissed in her direction. Sophia expelled a bolt of golden energy that mushroomed, flared and forged a violent shock wave, throwing the she-devil off guard. Its entourage stepped back, confused.

"Cowards," it hissed at its companions.

The she-devil drew all the energy in the room into herself and pushed it back at Sophia's. To Casey it all appeared to happen in slow motion. Its putrid smell, the screaming, its stretched mouth was closing. It thrust its claws forward and Sophia was lifted off her feet high into the air and slammed into the bookshelves. With its hand still extended towards her, as if to hold her back, it sucked Alex's spirit from his body, ingesting him. Sophia struggled against its force, rising up, and her necklace fell outside her shirt, catching the light: a blue laser beam magnificently struck the entity in its chest. It vanished from the room, taking Alex's spirit with it, leaving his little lifeless body behind. Casey, out of breath, helped Sophia to her feet. Daniel held Molly close to his chest.

Callie lowered Alex to the floor. Daniel checked his airways and felt for a pulse before commencing CPR. His face was beaded with sweat but he kept massaging Alex's chest for at least twenty minutes. He stopped and checked again for a pulse.

Kevin was crying, pleading with them to let him help, but his entreaties went unheard.

Daniel, emotionally and physically exhausted, stopped CPR. Callie got down on her knees and cradled Alex in her arms and cried out in pain. Casey didn't know what to do. He sent a bolt of energy at Alex's chest. His body jolted, but his tiny heart did not beat again.

Sophia leant into Casey and said, "We have to go. Tell Jade to get Kevin and Tim and meet us upstairs. I'll get Shaun."

Everyone was heading upstairs, giving Callie and Daniel privacy in their grief. Sophia whispered in Jade's ear to get Kevin and come upstairs.

Kevin lovingly held Molly. Casey's heart was aching for him. He knew what it was like to lose someone you loved. Daniel pried Alex from Callie's arms and lifted him up. He clutched him tight and buried his head in his chest and sobbed, walking listlessly into their bedroom.

Callie stroked Molly's cheek. "I'm afraid she'll fall asleep," she said to Amy through tears.

"If you like I can sit with her awhile," Amy said.

"No." Callie took Molly from Kevin's arms and hugged them both tight. She let go of Kevin and followed Daniel into their room.

Casey went up to Kevin and watched as his parents closed the door behind them. "Come on."

Sophia was holding onto his elbow. "Father." He had stopped praying and the crackling fire seemed intrusive and unwelcoming.

He pushed down on his knee to rise.

Sophia softly said, "We have to go."

He turned around and looked at her. He didn't want to leave, he wanted to pray and comfort the family.

"Come up to Casey's room when you're ready."

Casey saw the door handle turn. Father McDonald was breathing heavily. He saw Shaun slip his knife into his pocket. Casey busied himself packing his haversack and pretended he didn't see him, or Father McDonald come in to the room. Kevin was putting on boots and turned towards the door. They must have looked strange to Father McDonald, dressed in the middle of the night, ready to leave after what had just happened. They stopped when Father McDonald stepped into the room and cleared his throat.

Shaun was the first to speak. "Why is he here?"

"Why are any of us here?" Father McDonald said. "What's going on, Sophia?"

Sophia walked towards him and said, "We know how to get there."

"Now is not the time, whether you know how to get to Israel or not," Father McDonald said.

"Father, you have been with me from the beginning, and I can't do this now without you."

"He's right, I'm not going," Kevin said.

"We need to go now," Sophia said.

"Why now?" Kevin yelled. "My brother just died in his sleep for Christ's sake!" His faced screwed up with grief. The tears tumbled from the side of his eyes and he swallowed back the sobs. "Don't you care?"

"We have to go now, because of Alex," Sophia said. "The curtain between the two worlds is so thin we are losing our hold on this world. We will disappear and become the dead."

Very softly, Jade rubbed Kevin's back and Tim rested his hand on his shoulder. Kevin looked flustered; he pushed his hair back and wiped his face with his forearm. Casey continued to pack.

Father McDonald looked confused, puzzled. "You can't leave your families in their time of need."

Casey finished packing and watched Jade softly talking to Kevin. Whatever she said, it worked. Kevin brushed his hair out of his eyes as a ball of green energy expanded from his chest, pushing his shoulders back. Kevin stood tall, drew in a deep breath, widened his arms and exploded into life. Casey watched speechless as the room hummed and the floor vibrated under their feet. It sounded like a hole was ripping through the fabric of the universe.

"In God's name, what is that?" Father McDonald said.

A doorway began to open. The space before Kevin began to ripple. The atoms in the air ignited with light, creating a hole, separating time and space. The bay window could hardly be seen behind the transparent wall of light.

"Let's go, then!" Kevin said and ran into the wall. Tim, Jade and Shaun followed behind.

Casey threw his bag over his shoulder. "We have to go, Father," he said and gently held his elbow.

The priest walked up to the wall and touched it, quickly pulling away. "God help us."

"Have faith, Father. See the continuity," Casey said, guiding him forward.

Father McDonald stepped into the liquid light. He turned and looked back and Casey saw a rainbow bending around Father McDonald as if he were traveling at great speeds, then he disappeared from Casey's sight.

As Casey began to step into the liquid light, he heard the bedroom door open and saw Daniel walk in. It must have been a shock for Daniel to see half of Casey's body, then to see him completely disappear into the rippling mirage. Casey could feel hands reaching for him, pulling him into the parallel world.

They stood in silence. Father McDonald appeared to be enthralled by the luminous surroundings: an enchanted forest, everything pulsing with life. Casey couldn't help but watch Father McDonald gaze with awe into a clearing towards a garden and a sparkling pond. Scholars from different denominations were huddled together as if studying the secrets of heaven. A rabbi nodded towards Father McDonald, and a monk inclined his head before turning back to the other spiritual scholars.

"Are we in the Garden of Eden?" Father McDonald asked.

"I don't think so," Casey said. "I don't know where we are. We could be?"

"I feel no pain." Father McDonald flexed his hands, bent his knees. "My arthritis, it's gone!" He smiled widely, breathed deeply, drinking in the healing energy of the world. "It's a miracle, a place of miracles. We must be in heaven."

"We should call this place Athanasia," Jade said.

"What does that mean?" Casey asked.

"Timelessness. Everlasting life," Father McDonald said.

"Which way?" Shaun turned and faced Kevin.

Kevin looked around and saw the deer that had led him to Jade standing behind Shaun off in the distance. He stepped towards it and it disappeared.

"What?" Shaun turned, and looked behind him. It reappeared, standing with one foot forward. Shaun took a step, and the deer took a step.

Isn't she a beautiful translucent white? Kevin said in his mind.

Get out of my head, retard, Shaun thought, freaking out.

Sorry, I can't. It goes with the territory. They looked at each other with thoughts flying.

That's so weird, Shaun said, I feel like I'm buzzing.

"The deer's here for you, Shaun," Sophia said out loud.

"Me, why me?"

"You're the key to finding the Emerald Tablet. The deer came to me in the mountains," Sophia said.

"And when Jade needed help, the deer came to me," Kevin said.

"The deer is a symbol of my great-grandmother's spiritual path," Jade explained. "It represents mercy, certainty, and gentleness. My great-grandmother used to tell me the story about the deer. Sadly, today the deer is culled to prevent further damage to the environment; the skins are salvaged. To honor the deer's spirit Great Turtle made medicine drums with the skin and one day we made a drum together. On the pulse of the drum, she travelled through the sacred world to find and heal a person's ailments. She told me the deer can hear Great Spirit calling from the heights of Sacred Mountain. Great Turtle said the deer walked lovingly into the mist as a horrible demon blocked its way, trying to prevent it from connecting with Great Spirit; it told the deer to flee, that Great Spirit didn't want to be disturbed. But the deer felt no fear and graciously sought permission to pass, announcing its intention to journey to see Great Spirit. The deer was filled with love, gentleness and compassion for the monster that knew nothing other than to be a demon. The demon was curious how the deer lacked fear, trying and trying to frighten the deer, but could not. The deer's love pierced the demon's ugly heart, breaking the shell of its armor, and its heart thawed; evil shriveled up, turning into a pebble that lay in the dust at its feet. The beast stepped aside. The pathway was now clear for the deer to proceed up Sacred Mountain to Great Spirit."

The deer in front of Shaun turned and started to walk further into the forest. The foliage parted, creating a pathway as it walked. Shaun, enthralled, followed, and his companions followed him.

They walked deeper and deeper into the wondrous forest. In the aromatic air flew rainbow-colored birds with long tail feathers, and butterflies danced over the ferns. A variety of colorful fluorescent plants parted for them to pass. The light above beamed through the luscious canopy. *We're no longer under Earth's yellow sun, and here the sky is an endless electric blue,* Shaun thought. *My father was right.* The rich brown soil turned magenta as he walked, changing color with his personal heat signature. Petite yellow and blue, and some purple-winged, insects zipped in every direction.

"The Seal of Solomon!" Jade said excitedly. "That's it. That's the picture I've painted and have seen in my dreams for as long as I can remember. A green gate and a golden star; it's the Seal of Solomon. How could I not have seen it before?" The image flashed into everyone's minds.

"What does it mean?" Casey asked.

"We are bound to come across it. It is a key," she said.

A wall shimmered, just yards away, ahead of them and the deer walked straight into it, Shaun following, and one by one they all passed from the safety of the parallel world, the world of Athanasia, and into solid darkness.

Shaun dug in his pocket and pulled out his mini-torch and the small blue LED light. The atmosphere was suddenly hot and humid, the air thick and muggy. He heard Jade coughing. Beetles the size of a fist were scattered over the walls behind her. He decided not to tell her and tried ignoring the snakes that were slithering into the cracks in the walls. Shaun cast the light at the ground. They were standing on a dirt floor and there were iron rings bolted to the walls, chains hung loosely from them.

"This looks like a dungeon," Tim said. "Where the hell are we?"

"I don't know. Shh, someone's coming," Shaun said. They pressed themselves against the wall. There was nowhere for them to hide.

"Down here," whispered Father McDonald.

He looks pretty chuffed, Shaun thought. The old guy was holding up a heavy metal grille covering a hole, big enough for them to fit through. He had a grin across his faced that openly displayed his amazement.

"A gift from Athanasia," he said, jumping in, making a soft splash below. Father McDonald poked his head out of the hole. Sophia sat on the edge and jumped after him. Jade, not needing it, instinctively checked her pocket for her asthma puffer before following her. When they were all together, Shaun pulled the grating across, just as someone flicked on the lights.

Shaun heard a scuffle and a woman's moan, then a blow to a body and a thud to the ground. He twisted his head to see between the metal grates. He was just in time to see a leg and a boot lift up and pull back, swinging forward to kick the woman in the back. Shaun flinched, imagining her pain. It reminded him of his own actions, and the pain he must have caused others. He felt ashamed; a karmic mirror was being held up. *I'm looking at myself.* The woman curled and pressed herself against the wall protecting her head.

A deep voice, in heavily accented English, rumbled through the dungeon, saying, "You Americans are all the same." There was a third man standing on the stairs, his head hidden in shadows. His clothes were clean and stylish. He didn't walk down the final two stairs.

The voice was hauntingly familiar. "You have her blood. When you give us the formula, we will let you die quickly. You have wasted a whole year. If my family dies, your family dies!" He started to walk away, and then spun around, his fists clenched by his sides. "We found the woman, she is dead. Your serum is gone. My men saw her plane fall from the sky. You are stalling. No more. Tonight. It must be tonight. You give me the formula tonight, or tomorrow you die. No more games!"

He mumbled to the two guards in what Shaun thought could be Russian. Before the thug left, he turned back towards the woman and spat at her. Shaun recognized the men as the same guys who had arrived at the farmhouse, and had chased Kevin and Tim at the river. He was sure of it. Shaun signaled to Kevin to look and stepped aside.

Shocked, Kevin held his breath, his eyebrows raised and his mouth open, confirmation to Shaun that Kevin recognized them too.

Kevin mouthed. *But how?* He stepped aside, letting Shaun back in. Kevin whispered into Tim's ear, "It's the guys from the house."

The guards picked up the woman by the legs and arms like a lamb to the slaughter, and carried her down one of the many tunnels and out of sight. A loud metal door banged closed and echoed back to them. Keys jiggled, a click: the door was locked. Father McDonald had quietly moved through the water towards the next grate to see. The men suddenly stopped and looked in their direction. Shaun put a finger to his mouth and Father McDonald stopped. The men's elongated shadows disappeared with a flick of the industrial light switch. The dungeon was in darkness. The keys clanged again as the outer door was locked.

Jade whispered, "This tunnel system, canals from early irrigation, probably runs under the ancient buildings of the city. But what's a Russian doing in the Middle East?"

"What's anybody doing in the Middle East? Oil, probably," Shaun said. "I think I've met that man before."

"WHAT THE ..." Daniel ran across the bedroom and reached for Casey as he disappeared. Daniel was shocked, gingerly reaching his hand into the flickering light. It was a pleasant sensation, firing his neurons and stimulating his body. Daniel was spellbound. He could hardly see the far wall and boarded window. *Kevin, where are you, where have you gone?* Daniel thought and took a few steps backwards. He rocked on his heels and, then, like a long-jump athlete, sprinted into the membrane, jumping clear of the room and reality. He felt like an excited ten-year-old boy at a fairground, but also nervous like a weary old soul. *Take me to Kevin, take me to Kevin. Where are you, son?* Daniel saw within his mind's eye an image of Kevin surrounded by darkness and he could feel the pull of Kevin's energy. Daniel tumbled out of the comfort of the wall of light into the same darkness he had seen Kevin in. He felt cold and shivered. It was musty and he could taste dirt and sand in the air. He looked back in the direction of where he began, but there was no bedroom, no shimmering wall. He knew he was not in the house.

"Kevin," he whispered. "Kevin." A little louder. "Casey? Kevin? Shaun?" Shining up between his legs into his face was a blue laser beam. Blinded, he stepped back, covering his eyes. He could hear the sound of scraping metal. He backed up a little further and hit a wall. He put his hands out behind him and something crawled over them. He pulled his hands away and lost his balance, falling against the wall. Crunching the crawling things against his back. He jumped away from the wall, vigorously shaking his shoulders and arms, making sure nothing was crawling over him.

"Dad," Kevin cautiously whispered. "Dad, is that you?"

Shaun moved the torchlight up to the ceiling.

A woman's voice echoed in the dungeon. "Hello? Hello?" The silence made it sound as if she was shouting.

Shaun and Kevin climbed out of the sewer.

"Kevin," Daniel said. "Where are we?"

"Shh, if she hears us, maybe they can too," Shaun said. "We have to go."

"Who is she?" Daniel asked. "Where are we? What's going on?" "Hello?

Help me — they'll kill me — don't leave me here."

"We have to go," Shaun said and headed back to the

tunnel. Kevin grabbed his arm and stopped him from moving.

"We can't leave her," Kevin said. "I don't know what's going on, but we can't leave her crying for help."

Daniel could hear a commotion: Casey and Sophia were preventing Jade from climbing out of the sewer tunnel.

"Where is she, Kevin? Where's the woman?" Daniel said.

Shaun shone the torch, illuminating the tunnel's entrance. "Down that way."

Daniel scanned the area. There was little light. An explosion outside rocked the area and sand and rocks were dislodged from the ceiling, hitting them on the head.

"What the heck is going on up there?" Daniel said.

"Hurry, this way quickly." Shaun led them down the tunnel the woman had been carried.

They held their arms up, shielding their eyes and heads from the falling sand and rocks, past rows of empty cells. Shaun waved the light back and forth, searching for the woman. In the second last cell, crouched, hiding in the far corner, was the woman. Her face was buried in her arms. Shaun focused the light on her face, but she didn't move.

"Point it up, Shaun," Daniel said. He pulled on the bars. The door was sealed with an old chain, a shiny new lock. "Do you know where the keys are?" he said to Kevin and Shaun.

"They took them," Shaun said.

Daniel looked around for something to bash against the lock. He picked up a rock, holding it above his head.

"Wait! They'll hear," Shaun said. "I think I can ... I think I can do this. Here, hold this." He gave Kevin the torch. Shaun pulled out Casey's pocket knife and used it to start working on the lock.

"Come on, hurry up," Kevin said.

"Shut up," Shaun said. A click broke the silence. The woman's hair had been hacked off, leaving uneven chunks. She lifted her head, and her face was a swollen bloody mess.

Someone was running towards them down the dark tunnel. Shaun, Kevin and Daniel turned to see who was coming. Kevin swung the touch around. It was Jade. Casey was close behind, trying to stop her, grabbing her shoulder. She shook him off.

"Get off me, get off me."

Daniel caught Jade. "What's going on?" Daniel said.

"That's my mom."

"Jade." The woman had turned towards them, trying to see through her swollen eyes. "Jade! Jade! Is that you? Jade?"

"Mom!" Jade cried. Shaun finished picking the lock and removed the chain as fast as he could. Jade pushed him out of the way and burst into the cell.

Daniel stepped in, watching them cry in each other's arms. Her mother's dirty, bloody hands were running over Jade's body, hardly believing she was real. Daniel helped them up. "We have to go. Ellen, can you walk?"

"Who are you?" the woman said. "How do you know my name?"

"Don't be frightened, Ellen. It's Daniel, Callie's husband." "They said she was dead. I am so sorry, it's my fault."

"She's not dead. She's fine," Shaun said. "Can you walk?"

"Who's that?"

"Ellen, I am going to help you up," Daniel said. 'Help me, Shaun." Together they got Ellen to her feet and Daniel put her arm around his neck.

"Guys, how do we get out of here?" Daniel said.

"This way." Shaun led them back to the grille leading underground.

"No, I mean, home. How do we get home?"

"We can't leave for home yet. In here," Shaun said, letting Casey jump into the sewer first, followed by Kevin. "Get in, Jade." Shaun jumped in after her and Daniel lowered Ellen gently down to the others in the sewer. Father McDonald was at Shaun's side, helping him ease Ellen into the murky water.

Shaun searched his pockets for his lighter. "Give me your knife?" he said to Casey. "Forget that, I've got it." Shaun ran the flame over the blade and placed his hand on Ellen's head to hold it still.

"What are you doing?" Ellen asked.

"Relax. Courtesy of my dear old dad, I have had to do this to myself a dozen times." Quickly, he made a little slit in Ellen's swollen eyelids and the built-up blood spilt out.

"Thanks, I can see a little better now. How did you find me, Jade?"

"By accident. We're here for an artefact," Shaun said. "And we have to get moving."

Jade wrapped her arms around her mom. "I'm sorry, Mom."

"We are searching for the Emerald Tablet. What formula do they want?" Sophia said.

"Callie and I stumbled across a protein that allows metastasizing cancerous cells to revert back to healthy cells, as if there was no cancer at all. We found it by accident. We tested the virus with the samples and it too reversed, transforming into healthy cells. We watched the virus battle and we thought it was going to win, but it didn't, hence the protein's usefulness as a vaccine for the virus. Somehow, that Russian upstairs, who thinks he is a god, found out within days. I can only presume a government leak. And then I was kidnapped. He set up a lab here for me to replicate the experiment, but I couldn't make it work. There was a key element I can't replicate, but he wouldn't believe me. He wanted the vaccination for his family, and for blackmail purposes. He is greedy and is going to hold what's left of the world, hostage. He said all those who had worked in my lab at home were killed. I thought Callie was dead. Over the months I gave them what I could to stay alive. They brought in two pints of blood, saying it was Jade's. At first, I didn't believe them, but they said they would drain her whole body if I didn't do what they wanted. The blood was proof of life. I asked them to let me test it. If it was your blood, I would know. I'm sorry they did that to you. They didn't know how close they had actually come to the missing ingredient. He sold a vial of the experimental vaccine a few days ago for fifty million dollars, but it didn't work. The buyer's family died, hence the bombing, I think, and probably the twenty-four hour deadline." She coughed and choked on the words, wiping blood from her mouth. "He has the Emerald Tablet. He is missing pieces, though, and can only enter the underworld, the world of the dead. He can't find the missing pieces to activate the door to al-mawet."

"What does that mean?" Sophia said.

"No death," Shaun finished for her.

"It's from the Book of Proverbs," Ellen said. "The spelling varies within different religious texts, but they all have the same meaning. *Mawet* means death, *al- mawet* is 'no death'." Ellen held Jade close to her and said, "I am so glad you are safe. I would never have told him what the missing element is, never." She looked into her daughter's eyes.

"My blood — that's the missing element, isn't it. But

how? Is that what you wanted to tell me the day before you were kidnapped?"

"You *were* listening," Ellen said.

"I'm sorry, Mom."

"I hate to break up the family reunion but, seriously, we have to get that tablet. Do you know where he keeps it?" Shaun said.

"I'm with Shaun on this one," Tim said. "I really want to get out of this hellhole."

"I think so. It is in his private rooms," Ellen said.

"Is there a sofa, like a daybed, in the foyer outside four rooms with enormous wooden double doors?"

"Yes, that's right, but how —" she said. "Never mind, you can tell me later. We should go that way." She pointed into the darkness of the sewer tunnel.

The canal shook and Sophia fell into the water. Tim helped her up. Jade screamed as more explosions came closer and closer. They ran down the tunnel covering their heads. Daniel supported Ellen and she leant heavily on him. Her ankle was the size of a softball, but she didn't complain.

7

DESTITUTE: ENGLAND

It had been two days since they last saw Daniel, Father McDonald and the children. Joe tossed mixed powdered eggs into the pan, while Terry opened a can of breakfast juice. Amy handed Callie the baby's bottle and sat between Callie and Sally at the kitchen table. Kath stroked the golden retriever's head; Lucy was guarding the back door, preventing anyone from leaving. They had searched the grounds for two days, until the iron-cloud hung low, covering the sky above them for miles, forcing them to stay indoors. The wind began to howl and the trees were moaning, starting to splinter. The outside shutters clapped against the walls and the gale wailed through the seams of the house, but she was a solid old girl and was holding her own.

It's hard trying to attend to basic needs with the wee hen and her pals gone. She must have found a way, Joe thought. The timing was bad, with the young lad taken from them by the she-devil. They had laid Alex in Father McDonald's room.

Terry, Amy, Callie, Sally and Kath sat around, waiting to be picked off. Joe poured the eggs into the big dish for everyone to share. "Come on, people," he said, "you must keep up your strength. They are going to be okay. You said, Callie, that Kevin and Tim had done a disappearing act before. Look on the bright side: this time Daniel is with them. We have to be prepared for —"

"Prepared for what?" Callie said. "Prepared to die, is that it? We are all going to die? The last time the dead showed themselves, we were trapped in limbo for over four hours, Joe. They roamed freely for over four hours. The dead will walk the earth and we will fade into nothingness."

"Come on, Callie," Amy said.

"Don't 'come on Callie' me. I have lost both my sons and my husband. What do you know about loss?" Joe could see the hurt in Amy's eyes, telling him she knew only too well about loss.

"You're right, I don't know," Amy said.

Callie's raised voice frightened baby Molly and she started to cry. Callie jiggled Molly in her arms and said, "I'm sorry, Amy. I am so tired. I miss Alex, I miss Daniel and Kevin."

The dog scrambled to her feet and howled. Joe heard the outside shutters being ripped off and flying, crashing onto the roof. The windows shook violently. The boards split and pushed from the windows into the living room. It sounded like a jumbo jet was landing. The ceiling cracked above them, collapsing.

"Quickly, into the basement," Terry said.

Joe, the last one out, pulled the door closed just as the gas stove ignited into flames. He was thrown down the stairs backwards, landing hard on the ground with the wind knocked out of him. He pushed the door off himself, and crawled over to Terry.

"This way," Terry said, grabbing the torches and pushing

Sally and Kath through the hole in the wall. "Come on, Joe." Terry helped him to his feet and gave him a torch.

Joe didn't want to be back in the tunnels. He knew what lay ahead: darkness. He didn't want to be buried alive, but he needed to protect the others and he followed as they all moved deeper and deeper into the tunnels and the sounds of the evil storm faded.

8

DELIVERANCE: EGYPT

The smell wasn't too bad. The sound of dripping water in the sewer tunnels increased, signaling they had arrived at a junction and the main tunnel stopped. Four openings drizzled water into the main chamber.

"Where to now?" Shaun asked.

"I think it's that tunnel there," Ellen said, pointing.

"Really?" Tim said. "There's hardly any room in there."

"Stop complaining," Shaun said and climbed into the narrow space. One by one they followed with Daniel coming at the end.

Muffled voices could be heard up ahead. Everyone stopped. Shaun whispered to Casey. "Tell everyone to back up to the last opening and wait there."

"What?" Jade said.

"Back up, go back," Casey said.

"Don't have to tell me twice to vacate this entombing space." Tim said.

Alone, Shaun pushed his index finger against his nostril and blew the accumulated dirt from his nose. Slithering on his belly, his elbows and forearms became raw and tender. He kept moving closer to the muffled voices up ahead, and saw an air vent. Sound and air filtered between the copper slats. He peered out and looked straight into the head honcho's private suite, sparkling with gold, silk and other elegant materials. A spectacular room, in the center was a golden stand with an angled tabletop. An old familiar slab of rock was displayed upon it: the Emerald Tablet. It extended over the edges of the stand and exuded a green glow.

Boom! The tunnel around him shook, dislodging dirt over Shaun. He coughed and held his hand tight against his mouth, smothering the sound. He was scared he was going to be buried alive just like Rachel. The man was yelling in Russian and waving his arms around. His eyes were black shadows set deep into their sockets. His skin had yellowed. *He looks like a raving lunatic.*

"You! In one hour bring me the American woman, and you bring me the girl, the thief, now! This night of judgement I *will* sit beside the prince of darkness and rule this world."

Shaun wriggled backwards, to join the others.

"It's him, your kidnapper," he said. Ellen moaned. She looked worse than he even had after one of his dad's drunken rage attacks, but she didn't complain. "We don't have much time. He has sent for you, Ellen. The tablet is there, too. It's on a golden stand. The vent is way too small for us to fit through. We have to get into that room now."

"K, we have to get my mom out of here. She needs healing."

"No one is going anywhere till we get that artefact."

"I can do it," Kevin said.

"Do what?" Daniel asked.

"Get us into the room."

"How?"

Jade piped up to say, "He can bend space and time. That's how. How do you think you got here?"

"I can't bend time. I don't understand what it is that I can do. I don't create it, I think I just connect to it."

Daniel shook his head. "Connect to what? Forget it, there is no time. I'll go."

Sophia whispered, "No, no, you can't. Shaun has to."

The bombing had stopped again. Shaun was feeling really strange and edgy. The energy was exasperatingly itchy and he wanted to disappear. The confined space started to intensify everything. He saw Kevin nudge Tim. They were getting on each other's nerves. There was something in the air in the tunnel affecting them.

"I'll go with him," Kevin said.

Jade stood next to Kevin. Controlling her breathing, she grabbed his hand. Their combined energy encapsulated them, they sparkled and lit the tunnel like a swarm of fireflies. Shaun nearly had to shield his eyes. "What the hell?"

Kevin pulled away from Jade's grip, and the light went out. Kevin looked embarrassed and crawled into the tunnel. Shaun followed closely behind making sure he didn't cough and blow it. He waited while Kevin peered between the slats and studied the room before signaling to back up. They wormed their way back. Kevin stood and looked at him. "There is a window with drapes in the far corner on the other side of the room. We will enter there. The curtains will conceal us."

A low hum pulsed in the canal under his feet and up his legs. Shaun thought he could hear the sound of rustling trees. A transparent mercury window appeared. It completely covered the side tunnel entrance he had just wormed out of. Kevin looked at him with raised eyebrows, inviting him to go first.

He climbed through Kevin's window into the suite. The stale smell of cigar smoke was the first thing to hit him. He instantaneously felt a burning deep in his bowels. He was shocked at his own vulnerability and wanted to piss himself to cool down. The memories came flooding back. He felt weak at the knees: the smell, the nauseating cigars, the alcohol and laughter of that night; the tycoon, the buyer of the tablet victoriously slapping his dad on the back, praising him for the successful delivery. Shaun wanted to jump out from behind the drapes and beat the guy senseless. Kevin put a restraining arm across Shaun's chest as if he was aware of his urge, and shook his head and mouthed, *No!* Shaun stepped back and they continued to hide, waiting for their opportunity to snatch the Emerald Tablet.

The enormous doors to the suite were thrown open. A young woman was shoved into the room. She fell on her knees at the edge of a gold and black tapestry. Her veiled head hung low, eyes fixed on the rug beneath her. Her satin, lavender robe barely covered her body. Shaun wanted to grab the tablet and get out. He didn't know how much longer he could restrain himself. He wanted to kill the man. Clouds of anger burst into his mind; his head was aching, throbbing. A remote part of him knew he must wait. His temples felt so tight he was afraid his skull would rupture.

The man turned his back to the tablet and to the young woman. He appeared to glide across the room. He locked the doors and like a lion stalking its prey advanced on her and tore off her veil. Her hands went to her face. She kept her head down, her long wavy, dark hair concealing her features. Her movements somehow felt familiar and Shaun felt a jolt of déjà vu. The man put his hand on the young woman's chin and lifted her head up for a kiss. She avoided his lips and turned her head in Shaun's direction. Shaun stepped back in disbelief, holding his breath. He nearly fell into the shimmering waves and back into the tunnel. The man grabbed the young woman by the arm and pulled her roughly to her feet. He slapped her, knocking her down on the bed. The girl screamed and pulled out a knife from behind her. He slapped it away and laughed. She fell to the floor as the knife slid away. The tycoon dragged her up on her feet by the hair. She screamed, slapping at his arms. He pushed her face down onto the bed and seized her hips.

Shaun's mind and heart raced. It couldn't be, she looked the same as in his dreams. *It couldn't be. Is this all a dream? Another nightmare.* The man stretched out her arms, used her silk belt from around her waist to tie her wrists to the bed. She continued fighting and screaming, as her captor knelt on her to hold her leg still, but she still tried to kick against him. *Boom!* The building violently rocked and swayed on its foundations. He rose up and roared, yelled with each giant step he took towards the locked doors.

Shaun saw his opportunity and he knew it might be his only chance to save her. He ran out full of rage and jumped for the man's back. He felt Kevin grapple for his arm just before he went beyond the curtains. Shaun hoped the element of surprise was enough and leapt onto the man's back, pounding his fist into his neck and head and pushing him into the door. Shaun's bottled emotions thundered through his fists. The man turned and twisted trying to shake him off and Shaun saw Jade bolt out from behind the curtains. Her bracelet glowed. Shaun would have sworn he saw strange patterns spiraling from the bracelet like a holographic image projected towards the tablet as she grabbed it. Underestimating its weight, she nearly dropped it.

Shaun dug his fingers into the man's eyes. Kevin raced across the room, picked up the knife and hacked at the silk binding, giving it back to the young woman to tie around her waist. Shaun felt the tycoon's firm hands pulling him over his shoulder and slamming Shaun to the marble floor. Shaun felt happy. He couldn't remember the last time he actually felt this good. He smiled. Kevin opened the drapes for Rachel; she was safe. It took seconds, and that's all they needed. Jade clutched the Emerald Tablet to her chest and jumped straight into the translucent waves. Shaun could see that Kevin was waiting for him, keeping the doorway open. *He had left this kid for dead, and he still cared,* Shaun thought, as he elbowed the tycoon's face and watched the man's nose shift across his face in an odd way. He screamed and stumbled backwards. Shaun peeled himself off the floor and lunged for him, wrapping his arms around his neck from behind. The bloodied man ran backwards, smashing Shaun against the wall. Shaun let go and slid off the tycoon's back onto the floor, gasping for air. He felt like a goldfish out of water. The man's eyes had turned liquid black; Shaun knew he was about to die. He was okay with that — he was ready to die knowing Rachel was safe.

Rachel, he said in his mind, and smiled as she appeared from between the drapes. The room and the violence disappeared as he locked with her beautiful green eyes. Kevin pulled her backwards into the shimmering liquid and she was gone.

The man smashed Shaun in the face again and again, but Shaun didn't feel a thing. Seeing Rachel's smile instantly took him back to that day his father had stolen the tablet. He was a lifetime away, staring into her beautiful green eyes for the first time, and seeing her in her dress and boots sliding under the truck. He remembered the tablet and how heavy it felt. He started to come back to the present. He had flipped over onto his stomach and could feel the gemstones in his pocket digging into his side bringing him all the way back to the present and the pain. He was being kicked, stomped, and screamed at in Russian, Egyptian or Arabic, Shaun didn't know any more. What he did know was the tycoon was releasing his unbridled fury to break every bone in his body. He didn't care. Rachel was safe.

He felt consciousness slipping away. The kicking stopped, his head stopped hurting, he couldn't hear anything. It was quiet. Six wings unfolded before him. They opened up from the feet, the torso and then the face, an angel moving closer, his mother by its side. She too had the beckoning light of an angel. She reached out to him and he reached for her. Suddenly he was drifting; she was getting further and further away. He spiraled out of control, falling, her voice softly whispering in his ear, "I love you, I am so proud of you." And then she was gone.

A blast of pain erupted behind his eyes. His whole body screamed. Daniel was carrying him over his shoulders. The tycoon was struggling to his feet. Shaun, unaware of what had happened, found himself dangling over Daniel heading for the drapes. He tried to open his eyes. The man was on his feet, rushing in their direction. Shaun could taste the filth of the sewer mixed with the blood in his mouth, but his body no longer ached. The room had disappeared. Kevin closed the portal and the tycoon smacked hard into the stone wall, knocked unconscious. Daniel eased him off his shoulder as if he would still be riddled with broken bones, but he didn't feel a thing. He was healed again. He was starting to feel like the cat with nine lives. Rachel was standing with Jade's mom, fussing over her. *They apparently knew each other,* he thought as he watched her crying and laughing.

Ellen told her not to fuss and said, "So this is the knight in shining armor you said one day would come for you?"

Rachel turned to Shaun. "Yes, yes it's him," she said smiling.

Shaun looked at Daniel and offered his hand and Daniel shook it. "Thank you."

"I wasn't going to leave you behind."

"We need him," Sophia said.

Shaun ignored her and walked over to Rachel. She embraced him so tightly, he couldn't remember the last time he was truly hugged.

"We have to go back to the cave," she said in his ear.

"I know. You told me in a dream."

Kevin cleared his throat and said, "Which way to the cave?" Kevin moved next to Shaun and said, "It won't hurt," and placed his hands on either side of his head.

"How do you know it won't hurt?" he said, feeling awkward.

"I don't know, I've never tried this before. What else I am going to say? I am learning as we go."

And before Shaun could react, Kevin pulled his head slightly down to his and they touched foreheads. They looked like two Eskimos touching noses in greeting. The energy abruptly stimulated Shaun's forehead sending a weird sensation into his skull. It gave him a buzz before setting his nerves on fire. He felt his brain smoking like a motherboard with a burnt-out chip.

"Think of the cave, Shaun, not frying computers."

Shaun focused, letting Kevin hijack the image and then he let go.

"I think I've got it," Kevin said.

Shaun wanted to see if the tycoon was actually dead. While everyone was focused on Kevin, he crawled up the tunnel and peered through the slats of the vent. The man was alone in the room, lying unconscious on the floor by the window. The doors burst open and guards ran into the chamber. The window exploded, glass rained upon them and the side of the building started to fall. The tunnel was caving in. Gravity pulled Shaun over the edge into the room, but he felt hands latch onto his lower legs, holding him back, pulling him into the tunnel.

"We have to go," Casey yelled over the noise.

"What gives you that idea?" Shaun shouted.

Casey and Daniel helped Ellen to her feet. Father McDonald had been scanning the letters etched onto the Emerald Tablet. He flipped it over and there was an image of ten circles joined together by lines.

Shaun took it from him and shoved it into Kevin's backpack. "You can study it later. This place is going to come down."

"K," Jade said, "send my mom back. Get her out of here."

"She's right, Kevin," Daniel said. "Let's go home, all of us."

"Okay, Dad. Stand over there and imagine Casey's bedroom." Shaun watched Kevin create an opening big enough for Daniel and Ellen.

The ceiling started to crumble around them and Kevin yelled. "Go, Dad, go now." Daniel and Ellen had no time to react as Kevin pushed them into the portal and closed it behind them.

THE TUNNEL WAS FALLING APART. Kevin put his arm protectively above his head and focused his attention on creating another portal to the cave of Shaun's memory. He was having trouble opening a doorway. He was tired; he needed to feel the sun's rays. He remembered the day riding on his bike basking in the summer sun; it seemed so long ago, and it had recharged him as if he was a solar panel. Over the past few days he had used up so much energy and now it was catching up. He felt depleted, and desired to be full again, to be illuminated by the light, energized. He sensed Sophia looking at him and he shrugged and managed a stupid smirk and said, "I can't." She turned away and looked at Casey. *Sometimes those two seem to communicate without opening their mouths,* Kevin thought. He felt Jade touch his fingers and clutch his hand; he felt sparks fly between them. Casey snatched up his other hand, then he reached for Sophia's, and she reached out to Father McDonald who joined hands with Rachel. Shaun reluctantly reached out to Tim. They united in a circle and the energy raced into Kevin. They were all illuminated in a brilliant radiant warm light. The tunnels collapsed around them as they disappeared and they descended into darkness.

Shaun felt the hard ground beneath his feet and let go of Tim's sweaty hand. He reached into his pocket and pulled out his torch. "It's darker than I remember," he said to Rachel. It was hot and musty with a terrible stench. His skin crawled, he couldn't help scratching. He moved cautiously, thinking the caves might be saturated with the virus. He preferred to think of it as a virus, rather than the horrifying memory that was pushing into his mind. The thought was making him queasy and he felt flushed. He pulled off his sweatshirt and gave it to Rachel to wear.

Rachel took the jumper, turned it the right way and pulled it on.

"It's darker and the smell is stronger," Shaun said.

"Because the entrance is blocked. Your father blew it up remember?"

"I remember."

"There is a story of a secret entrance," she said and slipped the satin gown down around her waist to create a skirt.

Shivers raced up his spine. "It's the same as last time." A faint haunting sound of a bellowing horn could be heard from above. "That sound," he said.

"It's ten years to the day," Rachel said. "It is not coincidence. The master was complaining much about the thousands flocking to Israel, despite his attack. That sound is calling to the terrestrial courts: the lights of Earth are now hidden, and the gates of heaven have been closed. Today is the day of judgement for all mankind."

Shaun saw Father McDonald eyeballing the Emerald Tablet, and asked, "What are you staring at?"

"The writing looks Aramaic, an ancient language." He looked at Rachel and said, "They pass like sheep, one by one. The Lord looks from heaven; he beholds all the sons of men. From the place of his habitation he looks upon all the inhabitants of the earth. He fashions their hearts alike; he considers all their works. God understands all of our actions and today will make judgement upon us."

"What are you talking about?" Shaun said, agitated.

"Yes, you're right, holy man." Rachel stepped closer to him and said, loud enough for them all to hear, "Above ground, the people are meditating on the sound. It's the sound of the shofar; that was the first of one hundred and one blowings, so we maybe only have a little over an hour until the final sounding of the horn. It will reach the heavens and awaken the highest patriarchs this world has ever been blessed with in life and death, so they may bestow good judgement on mankind. The war between the good and bad angels has ceased and if the court is in session the heavenly angels and the prince of darkness are reading from the Book of Life. All our actions have been recorded from this life and past lives. Satan is rubbing his fire sticks together, counting our souls, ready to take control of what's left of Earth."

Shaun nervously moved his feet as she searched his eyes.

"Shaun, we must close the gate that our fathers opened before the last sound is blown. Then mankind will be blessed by God. He will send his mercy and give us the strength and courage to heal the world, to live in a state of immortality. The negative angels are winning so we must move fast. We don't have much time."

Shaun could see Tim shuffling closer and listening as everyone did. Tim cleared his throat.

"That reminds me," Tim said. "It reminds me of a 'Doctor Who' episode — when the world needed to think the same thing to bring his consciousness back. They need to reach a critical mass."

"This is no TV show — this is reality, the world is dying."

"Okay, keep your bra on! I get that. But because I saw that episode I sort of get what you're saying, and I am just saying that I get what you mean."

"I'm tired, sorry." She struggled to remember the boy's name.

"Tim," Shaun said for her.

Shaun had an epiphany, realizing in that moment that they were all meant to be here together. He knew that now.

"Certainty," Sophia said. "We need to be certain. Rachel, you said they were meditating, not praying?"

Rachel respectfully bowed her head slightly to Father McDonald. "Sorry Father, forgive me. Most prayers are like a shopping list of what people want. We hear our own voices. Meditating is listening for the voice of God."

Sophia was leaning against the wall and pushed herself off. "This time there is no second chance. We can do this. We need to have trust and certainty. We can imagine a new reality, take action and live it."

"It's all in the mind," Jade added. "Everything starts with a single thought. Nothing can exist, unless someone thought of it first. We create our futures, good and bad, and we have the power to change it. Free will."

Tim said, "K can do that. Can't you, K?"

FATHER McDONALD STUDIED the tablet and the ten scripted points. Rachel propped herself against the wall and sat watching the holy man. Sophia and Casey were sitting beside her. The priest did not wear his sacred garments or a cross around his neck, but everyone called him Father. The tablet was obviously hefty for his ageing arms. The metal side of the breastplate glowed upon his face. She looked closer and saw the images on the emerald side. *Channels like pathways joining at circular junctions; the Tree of Life.* Rachel stood and dusted herself off and knelt in front of the holy man. She studied the partly concealed markings: three columns. The two outside columns had three circles each, and the inner column had four. They were connected by parallel lines, like pathways, and she counted twenty-two. Rachel saw the image as two kites end to end and a square in the middle separating them. It looked like an elaborate highway system.

"What are you doing?" Father McDonald asked. "I have been trying to focus on understanding the writings and relate them to the scriptures, but Rachel, your intensity was so acute I couldn't concentrate on anything but your presence."

"I am looking at the drawing on the back," she said, opening up her hands waiting for him to give her the tablet. "May I see it? I risked my life to find that."

He looked at the script one last time and passed the tablet to her. It weighed heavily in her hands and quickly she lowered it to the floor of the cave. *This is what my father died for,* she thought, tracing her fingers over the images. Rachel felt Kevin and Jade move closer, watching her dig away some of the dirt with her fingernail to reveal deep etchings as wide as her small finger. They weren't simply parallel lines, because in between them were symbols. "This symbol," she said tapping the Emerald Tablet with her finger, "is the letter (א) Aleph," she said. "It's —"

"I know what it is," Father McDonald said, irritated. "It's the first letter of the ancient language of the Aramaic and Hebrew alphabet, and that one on the left side is (ב) Bet."

"Who has water?" she said.

"I do," Tim said. "I was saving it." Tim wiped the dirt off his face that was being irrigated by his own sticky sweat. "It's hot and I really wanted to drink it." He pulled it out of the backpack and handed it over to Rachel reluctantly. "You can have it."

Rachel swished the crystal clear water, assessing the amount, and saw Tim lick his lips waiting for her to take a sip, anticipating it. He was probably imagining it hitting the back of his mouth and sliding down his throat. She could imagine he would have pumped it between his cheeks first and just before the coolness subsided swallowed it. He was going to be sadly disappointed.

Rachel pulled her sleeve over her hand and used it as a rag. She scrubbed away the dirt that concealed parts of the image. She twisted off the lid and poured a little over the back of the Emerald Tablet.

Tim yelled. "What the hell? I thought you wanted to drink it. Fair dinkum, there was no way I would have given it to you if I had known you weren't going to drink it!"

Ignoring him, Rachel poured the rest over her sleeve and continued to clean the tablet. She moved from the top circle across to the one on the right and then left, and continued until she had cleaned every circle and line to reveal letters and symbols. Satisfied they were as clean as she was going to get them under the circumstances, she went back to the first and tried to read the markings.

Her eyes lit up. She remembered when her father was alive she would hear him rise in the middle of the night, and sit with a pale light that might as well have been a candle, to study a book that had this very image on the front cover. He would rock back and forth as if to the rhythm of a song only he could hear. Just before dawn, he would close the book and turn off the light. Sometimes she would fall asleep outside the room and he would gently lift her, hoping not to wake her, but even with his gentle touch he did. She kept her eyes shut tight, pretending, as he carried her back to her bed. Neither of them spoke about it. Each time he found her, he would put her back into bed.

"Look, Shaun, look," she said, excited.

Shaun looked at her fingers covered in dirt and blood and he looked into her eyes and back at her hands. A few of her nails had broken, exposing tender flesh. He couldn't help wondering at the struggle for freedom she must have endured. She was so beautiful she should be dancing in the sun, not crawling around dark, evil caves.

"Do you understand the symbols?" he asked.

"Yes, I think so, this means keter — the crown or divine spark." She traced over the three arches above the first circle, keter, and said, "I think it means limitless light: infinite or endless. I can't be sure."

"The two pillars — on the right and down the bottom it reads jachin, the pillar of mercy. The left says boaz, the column or pillar of severity, judgement."

"Doesn't jachin relate to King Solomon and boaz to King David? Tell us what you can in chronological order," Father McDonald said. "Go back to the top and start again, Rachel."

She breathed out heavily. "Um, um um um ..."

"Just relax." Father McDonald said.

Rachel started to cry.

"Why are you crying?" he asked.

"I don't know." Jade rubbed her back and Casey and Sophia moved closer and placed a hand on each of her knees and balanced her energy. She started to relax, took in a deep breath, sniffed back the tears, and breathed out and said, "Okay."

"This one is Keter," she said and trailed her finger down along the right pathway to "Chochmah" and moved her fingers across the inner line, creating the first circle on the left. "Binah." She moved back to right column circle and called out "Chesed" and back to the left. "Gevurah", then back to the right, but this time there was a circle dipped in the middle. "Tiferet." She continued to move from right to left. "Netzach and Hod," and passed down to a third inner column circle, "Yesod, righteousness." Quickly, she moved down to the final inner circle, tapped it and said, exhausted,

"Malchut manifestation. It's the Tree of Life, the three-column system, the balance between mercy and judgement."

Father McDonald said, "The channels of the descending divine light and the ascending returning light."

Jade knelt behind Rachel, nearly placing her chin on Sophia's shoulder so she could follow Rachel's finger across the tablet.

"The pathway," Jade said, reaching over and touching it, "has three symbols. I gather from what you said before, Rachel, that this one is an Aramaic or Hebrew letter. I can tell you that this symbol represents a planet, and this squiggle represents an astrological house. Look at the second circle on the middle column. What did you call it?"

"Tiferet," Rachel said.

"Tiferet has the symbol of the sun, a planet. And this symbol," Jade said, tapping the tablet, "represents east, and this symbol represents air."

Rachel jumped in then. "And this says Uriel, the angel. And this one, Chesed. This says Michael. It must be the Archangel Michael."

Jade said, "In the circle you called Chesed is the symbol for Jupiter, water and south."

"It means mercy," Rachel said. "Chesed is mercy."

Father McDonald held his hand over his chest as if in pain and looked at Rachel. "We have ten understandings, starting with the divine spark, right? Then wisdom, under-standing, mercy, judgement, harmony, victory, splendor, righteousness and manifestation, and there are twenty-two pathways, twenty-two letters. Ten circles, four directions, four angels — Michael, Gabriel, Rafael and Uriel — twelve planets and twelve astrological signs. What does it mean? It's all mystical and meaningless."

"Why are you being so negative?" Sophia asked.

They all sat quietly. The cave was suffocating. The excitement of their new discovery was quickly disappearing. They struggled to decide what to do next. They lost interest in their quest and sat lethargically, separated, until they stopped communicating.

Father McDonald took the tablet off Rachel. He wasn't interested in the circles and lines, and flipped it over and continued searching for the meaning of the words on the shiny side. Rachel watched him for a while, then closed her eyes to sleep.

CASEY UNFOLDED his legs to stand up and move away from Rachel. His body shivered. Images hurried across the walls of the cave. He tried to focus, but all he could see were two children crying, and heading in their direction was a swarm of evil. The swarm scraped like metal against the walls and felt like thunder. Men screaming in pain echoed around the cave. Casey doubled over, squeezing his eyes shut, trying to block the raw images. His stomach somersaulted. He felt faint, and opened his eyes, and the cave spun anticlockwise. He held his hand out to balance against the wall. The coolness was welcoming on the palm of his hand, a single moment of relief — until every muscle in his body spasmed and cramped with fiery bolts of pain. He was frozen, unable to control his body. His mind plummeted into the darkness of the cave, and the vortex that was sucking the life out of the world was here, it was everywhere. He didn't know how to separate himself from it. He could feel the devil on his back and the internal heat was unbearable. He struggled to scream, but like in so many of his nightmares, he was powerless to escape. Casey's body was thrown into convulsions.

"Don't touch him," he heard Kevin yell.

"Sophia, is he epileptic?"

"No. I think he has connected to the cave."

"What? Connected to the cave. What does that mean?" Father McDonald followed all the first-aid procedures, but Casey's body jerked out of control on the ground. Kevin scrambled down to lie beside Casey and hold his convulsing body. Casey felt Kevin holding him as tightly as he could. Sophia sat by his head and closed her eyes. He was watching everything from a distance.

"That's enough!" Father McDonald screamed. He was losing his cool. "It's time we all went home. This has to end." But no one listened, except Casey. He could hear him as if he was far, far away. Father McDonald began to pray.

Warmth surrounded him. He didn't know where he was; all he could feel was warmth. A rhythmic, calm breeze of words passed through his psyche, becoming louder. He focused on the sounds. He knew that voice. *I've got it*, he said to himself, *it's Kevin*. He felt an overwhelming sensation and saw a wash of psychedelic colors behind him; it was Sophia. Sounds of more voices flowed into his ears and his back began to hurt and suddenly a blinding light exploded behind his eyes. An angel took flight, and he tried to remember where he had seen it before.

9

MAZE OF MACHPELAH CAVE: HEBRON

Casey's eyelids sprang open, startling Jade, and he blinked repeatedly as he tried to see. He could only move his arms slightly because Kevin still had him in a bear hug.

"K, you can let go," Jade said.

Casey was eyeballing Shaun who had flicked on his torch. "I saw what happened when you two were kids," he said to Shaun and Rachel as he sat up. "You had nothing at all to do with what happened. You had no idea and you have protected the world ever since without even knowing it."

"I don't know what you're on about, idiot." Shaun moved away and searched for a way out.

"We can't go that way, Shaun," Sophia said, helping Casey up. "We will all die before we even get close. It's waiting for us. This battle has been foretold. We just didn't get the text. I think they have already begun to attack us. We have to leave or we'll die."

Shaun spun around and faced Sophia. He had a haunting smile. "You think you have all the answers."

"I don't know what you mean."

"Stop talking like you're some prophet. You're not a prophet! You're just some kid that has lost her family too. Attention seeker."

Jade looked at Kevin and said, "I don't feel so good."

Jade slid down the wall and cried.

"What's wrong?" Kevin asked, crouching beside her.

"I don't want to be here." Her head started to spin, the vertigo returned.

"None of us want to be here," Shaun shouted. "Don't you think I'd prefer to be at home? You think I've enjoyed being stuck with you retards. You think I want to be crawling around in this cesspool?" He spat on the ground.

Jade started to sob. Shaun walked away rubbing his head, looking confused.

"What the hell? Why are you crying?" Tim asked Jade.

"Back off, Tim," Kevin said.

"Piss off, Kevin. I'm sick of you telling me what to do. She's a pain in the ass."

"Oh, the lovers are having a falling out," Shaun said. "Could he be bi, after all? Oh Tim, what are you going to do? He doesn't love you any more."

"Shaun, don't be a dick," Kevin said, standing up.

Jade stopped crying and was looking around at everyone. Rachel was backing away from Shaun, as if she didn't know him. Sophia and Casey were still sitting on the ground and everyone was arguing. It was only a matter of seconds before they started to get physical with each other.

Sophia looked at Casey and said, "We have to get out of this cave."

All hell broke loose. Tim jumped on Shaun, screaming for vengeance, knocked him to the ground and slammed his fists into his face. Shaun flicked him off; Tim tripped over his own feet and fell onto Rachel.

Jade covered her ears and closed her eyes. She started to cry, feeling helpless. *They're all going to kill each other,* Jade thought. One, two, three, breathe in, one, two, three, breathe out ... she continued to count, chasing away the anxiety, hiding behind her hands, pressing them hard into the sockets of her eyes until she saw sparks of light. Images flashed in her mind: Sophia's necklace, then a swimming turtle, her bracelet, her great-grandmother's face and then her drawing of a door with a star, the Seal of Solomon, her green iron gate — *that's it!*

Jade slowly lifted her head trying not to vomit. She felt drunk, her speech was slurred. "I know." Tears streamed down her face. *Maybe I'm having a stroke,* she thought. This was a dream she had had all her life and now she could act on it, but she was about to blow a fuse. All her life the universe knew this day would come. The idea was profound; it wasn't logical, a paradox. "I know," she whispered a little louder, tilting her head towards Sophia and Casey. She couldn't be heard over the shouting. Jade dragged her leg from under her and stretched it out slowly towards Casey and touched his foot, trying not to move her heard, afraid she would vomit.

CASEY WAS FROZEN to the spot, watching the rage unfolding amongst them. Emanating from within the walls of the cave were dark angels. *I can feel them.* They were being smothered by the evil that was surrounding them. Suddenly he felt something brush against his foot and instantaneously Jade's emotions merged with his. The nausea was overwhelming and he vomited, his head spinning, Jade pulled her foot away and the spinning sensation stopped. He moved towards Jade. She was trying to say something, but he couldn't hear her. The energy was becoming thick like soup, it was hard for him to move. With all his strength he clapped his hands together and it was like releasing a mini atom bomb. The cave was momentarily filled with light and everyone was thrown back against the wall, winded and struggling for breath. They all looked at each other, shocked and embarrassed. Father McDonald dropped the tablet and Casey scooped it up and stuffed it in Kevin's backpack.

"What?" Casey asked Jade.

"I know where the secret entrance is."

Sophia shuffled on her backside closer to Jade and touched her knees.

"Don't move me or I'll be sick," Jade said.

Sophia crawled over and started rubbing her back.

"Stop." It was too late. She dry retched.

Jade moved her hand towards Kevin. Casey watched him slide his hand forward till their fingertips touched; liquid energy travelled between them, embracing them as one. He balanced her out. She looked up at him with an exhausted look. Sophia stood up and Kevin sat in her spot facing Jade. He closed his eyes and she opened her mind to him. They looked like one soul. Casey was in awe and he felt amazed and privileged to be seeing this. He looked at Sophia and smiled, knowing she too could see. Casey was a mixed bag of emotions right now and grateful for his new friends; they all seemed overwhelmed.

EVERYONE HAD their eyes on Kevin as he sat behind Jade, cradling her in his arms and crossing his legs over hers. Casey could see ripples in space opening up behind Kevin.

He tilted backwards holding onto her like a scuba diver dropping off the side of a boat. They merged into the membrane, out of the cave, disappearing into the coolness of the rippling mirage.

Casey was the first to follow, practically landing on top of Kevin and Jade who were still huddled together on the ground. Kevin looked up just in time to see Casey hitting his nose on a green iron gate with a golden star. Kevin was still holding Jade, and Casey believed they wanted to stay in the embrace longer than was strictly necessary.

It was night and hard to see. The air tasted salty as if near the ocean. Casey looked to see what was beyond the green bars and the stone courtyard opposite a window. On the left wall was an ancient carving of a maze. He picked up the shiny new padlock that was nearly as golden as the star: the Seal of Solomon. Kevin and Jade began standing up, patting the dirt off themselves. He noticed the gentleness Kevin had towards her. He pushed stray strands of hair off her face, and gently rubbed the side of her arm. Casey smiled, turning away to focus on the maze that was beyond the gate. He saw something move in the shadows behind the window. A loud male voice, not far from them said, "Ti ... kee .. ah!" followed by a bellowing that pierced into the dark of the night. Casey jerked, the horn was blown again, and it ignited every molecule of light in the atmosphere. It cut deep into his soul, and it echoed far into the sky. He spun around towards the horn and saw hundreds of lit candles being held towards the heavens. Tim crashed into Casey, twisting him at an odd angle, pushing his face back into the gate. He saw a shadow moving out of the corner of his eye again. Everyone poured through the opening, piling up against him and the green gate. He wanted to laugh at the situation. *This is probably what it's like in a mosh pit.* Casey's face was pressed against the smooth cool star, and he felt centered. There was none of the frenzy of a music concert. He had a sense of wellbeing, peace and harmony within the world. *Maybe I should become a spiritual teacher.* He wanted to remain like that forever. If anyone was watching, it might have appeared quite funny to see them all piled up together. Rachel was the first to step aside.

"I know this place," she said. "This is the Cave of Machpelah. This is the gateway for the light to enter into our world. It's the resting place of the world's greatest sages."

"We cannot enter!" Father McDonald said.

"I agree with the holy man," said Rachel. "This gate, the one with the star, is Jacob's resting place."

Jade put her hand on the star, and started to weep again. Her emotions were in overdrive. *She wasn't sad*, Casey thought, she was the complete opposite; she was full of joy and excitement as if she had drunk ten red energy drinks.

"This is my door," Jade said. "I have been dreaming of this door all my life."

"That's incredible," Kevin said. "And you have never been here before?"

"No, never," said Jade. "It's been a frustrating enigma. See over there," she said, pointing to the far right-hand side where a three-dimensional maze was carved into the wall. "That is the key to unlocking the passage that will take us directly where we need to go, I am sure."

"Did you dream of it too?" Sophia asked.

"No, but I just know it is. I have no logical understanding as to why or how I know, but I just know. Oh shit, I'm sounding like you guys."

"This is a holy place," said Father McDonald. "We can't desecrate it. God wouldn't want this." He held the bars in his hands and began to pray. "Forgive our trespasses ..."

Most of the people holding the candles, behind them, were facing away from them and concentrating on their connection to the light of God. Casey was in awe of the proceedings. He didn't think he had ever seen a mass of people so peacefully uniting for a common cause. There must be thousands of uninfected people. Casey could only see a small portion of one side, but it felt as if he was in the middle of a packed stadium. He turned back to the gate to see Shaun take the padlock in his left hand and start to pick it with his right. Father McDonald put his hand over his and said, "You can't, son. This is the way of thieves. There must be another way."

THE WIND PICKED up Rachel's hair and moved it across her shoulder. The golden candlelight, the symbols of peace, saturated the desolate terrain. Buildings were missing chunks of their walls. *My mother might be in the crowd,* she thought. Rachel stood on her tiptoes, searching. All the men were dressed in white, while the women were on the oppo- site side and strangely dressed in what could only be described as their "best". She couldn't remember the last time she had seen her mother or brother. She figured they must have given up searching for her a long time ago. She had told her brother her intentions and made him promise not to tell their mother that one day she would return with the artefact their father gave his life for.

Rachel saw Kevin out of the corner of her eye as he dropped his head. She turned to watch as he closed his eyes, breathing deeply in. The stone wall protecting the tomb of Jacob became concealed with a vapor-like mirage. Kevin opened his eyes and stepped through. Tim, Shaun and

Casey followed one by one, disappearing into the moving liquid. This was fantastic; she couldn't believe what Kevin could do. She had never seen it before.

It was strange seeing Shaun after all this time. He was more handsome than she had imagined. She had never stopped believing he would come back for her. *There was something magical woven tightly within the tragedy, for he has become so hardened and filled with pain, but still he fights*, she thought.

The moonlight was reflected in Jade's eyes. Rachel was mesmerized by Jade's bracelet — it was glowing. The etchings were rising up from the bracelet and the shapes were like letters from the Emerald Tablet. Father McDonald hesitated in front of her before going through the mirage, and he crossed himself, asking for forgiveness as he stepped across the threshold, followed by Jade. Rachel couldn't take her eyes off the bracelet. *Am I the only one seeing this?* She stood there for a few seconds watching the bracelet disappear and reappear on the other side of the locked gate. Rachel stepped into the membrane and followed. She turned back to peer through the gate, looking at the mass of people. Nobody seemed to notice them moving inside Jacob's tomb.

The maze looks a lot bigger on this side.

"Maybe we just need to find the right pathway and push it in, to activate a door," Tim said.

"It would have to be more complicated than that," Jade replied. "Otherwise it would have been discovered lifetimes ago."

Tim and Kevin slid down the wall and sat on the ancient stones and patiently waited. Rachel and Jade got closer to the maze. Both of them started running their fingers over the patterns.

"The markings were rising up out of the stone. They were geometrically at specific points representing the four elements," Jade said.

"It looks very much like Hebrew, but it's not," Rachel said. "I think it is, like on the tablet, the Aramaic language." She studied each letter and interpreted as best she could. "These represent the beginning and the division. There are twelve lines in the maze."

"What is the beginning and the division?" Kevin asked.

Father McDonald was flicking through his Bible and stopped. "In the Book of Numbers, Chapter Two talks about how the twelve tribe were broken into four groups of three from the center of the tabernacle into the east towards the rising sun; south, west and north."

Rachel ran her fingers over the lines and said, "The twelve tribes, the twelve houses of the zodiac, the four angels. Like the tablet, if this is a puzzle to be solved there are hundreds of combinations."

"What I see," said Jade, "is the squaring of the circle."

"There is no circle, Jade," Rachel said.

"If you put a compass in the center of the maze," she said, drawing it with her finger, "and line it up with the east, you can draw a circle touching each of these markings." She tapped the points. "Imagine all the lines are removed, leaving the four points. You have a circle inside a square. Sacred geometry, the drawing of the squaring of the circle, fits within this maze."

"Why is it significant?" Kevin asked.

"She isn't really talking to us, she is thinking out loud," Father McDonald said.

Jade ran her fingers along a line, out from the center square to the east. "Down to the south-east corner and followed back into the center, and out to the west and up to the north-west corner. Back into the center and out along the eastern line and up to the north corner, and back into the center out along the western line and down to the south. Now draw the outer line from the south to the east up to the north and around to the west, ending in the south, completing twelve movements," she said.

The rock face of the maze grinded like giant teeth as the stones started to move. It was coming to life. Inner sections moved back into the wall, and the lines Jade had drawn along scraped forward, and began to spin in a clockwise direction. The center point protruded about four inches from the rest of the structure. Jade reached out and pushed it back in. After the passing of the centuries, the long rectangular stone slab under their feet, as if on a spring, recoiled into life just like its designers intended on the day it had been created long ago.

Suddenly, like a rug pulled from under them, the stones parted and they tumbled into the dark shaft, screaming. The stone slab sprang back into position, silencing the sounds of their descent. Rachel dragged her nails along the stone wall, trying to slow her fall. They were jumbled together as they fell, hitting one another. Rachel felt her head connect with someone's shoe and was knocked unconscious just before she hit the bottom of the shaft.

10

TOMB OF THOTH

Kevin couldn't catch his breath, his lungs wouldn't expand. Finally, he drew in a breath and dirt filled his nostrils. Kevin coughed. The dirt went down into his throat; he started coughing harder, and then spitting. Not a stream of moonlight or starlight above; the darkness was absolute. Jade coughed in his face and Kevin reactively raised his hand. He sat still and listened. He could hear her coughing, and smelt her sweet odor. He reached out, and there she was. He let loose a sigh of relief. He felt her leg and left his hand upon it to comfort her. A hand gently lay upon his. At first he thought it was Jade, as it was soft, but also a little too big. It was Tim. "Tim, are you okay?"

"I'll be right. Look after Jade."

"Jade?" Kevin whispered. He thought it was best not to talk too loud. He could hear someone or something start to move.

"Sophia? Casey?" They didn't answer.

He reached for the strap of his backpack and lifted one side off. *Please don't be smashed, please don't be smashed,* he thought, as he slowly reached into the bag. The tablet was cold and rough around the edges, but it seemed to be intact. He tightened the straps again and opened up the front pocket, looking for a torch. It was gone, then suddenly a blue light lit up the area and it was Shaun with his little blue LED light. He was sitting against the opposite wall about four yards away. Next to him, Rachel lay unconscious and partly hidden underneath Father McDonald, who was himself bent at odd and hideous angles. Casey and Sophia tried to stand, wobbling as they did. Sophia's hair, which usually looked like golden silk, was matted with dirt and blood. Kevin watched as Jade strained to catch her breath. He put his hand on her shoulder and she held up her finger for a minute, reassuring him she would be okay while she continued to control her wheezing. Over her shoulder he saw that Tim, washed by the glow of blue light, had crawled over to Rachel. Together with Shaun, Tim gently moved Father McDonald off her. Father McDonald screamed in pain, then passed out. Rachel still wasn't moving. Shaun squeezed her shoulders gently, quietly saying her name.

Kevin went to Father McDonald's side. Rachel coughed. Kevin looked up and noticed Tim had left Rachel in Shaun's care as soon as she started to talk. He was by Sophia and Casey, trying to help them. Tim was moving from one person to another, quickly and deliberately, caring for everyone. He was totally in his element. He reminded Kevin of his dad. Tim ripped off his shoe and a sock and then put his shoe back on. *What's he doing,* Kevin wondered. Tim tied the sock around Sophia's head to stop the bleeding. *If the bleeding didn't kill her, the smell would*, he thought.

They were all a mess. Father McDonald's leg was twisted at the hip and his head was slumped to the side. His ear was bleeding, the blood dripping off his shoulder and onto the dirt floor. His hip and leg were broken.

Kevin scanned around for a doorway, an exit. It seemed they were in an alcove no bigger than a small shipping container, but beyond the entrance to their small space was a vast chamber that Shaun shone his pocket torch into.

Tim crouched on one leg beside Sophia, making sure the sock was doing its job and softly spoke to Casey. He pushed himself up and headed in Kevin's direction. *Who is this guy?* Kevin thought, watching Tim make his way over. "Need some help, K?"

"You can tell me where my mate Tim's gone for starters?"

Tim didn't answer. He scanned Father McDonald's body. "His leg is definitely broken. I know that angle," Tim said. "His hip reminds me of my grandma's when she missed the chair and fell. He is going to be in a lot of pain when he comes around."

A scream echoed through the chamber; Father McDonald was conscious. Jade squeezed her hands over her ears. The sound reverberated in the small space and the outer chamber erupted into life. Kevin felt his stomach churn. He began to sweat profusely and his breath became rapid. A three-tiered ancient platform, each level protected by a ring of molten flames, filled the chamber and his eyes. The sudden heat was scorching, and they tried to back away. Orange and yellow flames guarded the first set of twelve ancient steps that led to the first platform. The second level glowed with purple and blue flames, protecting the next set of twelve stairs that led to the third tier. At the top of the thirty-two steps, on the third tier, was a platform surrounded by white molten flames. Upon the platform four cubed columns stood in each corner, like centurions guarding an altar where a golden statue lay. The statue's head was odd and had a pointy, long arched nose like a beak. At the chest was a cavity. Something had been removed; a breastplate, the Emerald Tablet.

"It's a statue of Thoth," Jade said. She stood beside Kevin, each of them breathing shallow and rapid. "It's a bit like a sarcophagus."

Over on the far side of the chamber, a black whirlpool of expanding dark matter began to zap away Kevin's energy. He felt he was looking into the emptiness of the universe and felt overwhelming sadness. He could see something within the swirling darkness accelerating towards them. It started as a dense shape and broke free into the light of the cave. Translucent, it flapped and fluttered like a giant butterfly. As it got closer, Kevin thought, *that's no butterfly.* The translucent entity had razor-sharp teeth, the head of a bat and the tail of a scorpion. It flew over the flames, straight for them.

"Come to me!" Father McDonald yelled with sudden strength. The entity separated into hundreds of micro parts and went straight up Father McDonald's nose and in through his mouth. His eyes pooled with black tar and he gagged and choked. How he was even conscious Kevin didn't know, but the old man was fighting to stay in control of his body and soul.

Kevin couldn't help him. The dense whirlpool of negative matter had accelerated, drawing everything in towards it. Everything that contained a spark of light was being pulled into the stream of blackness. Kevin could feel the drag. The first and second set of flames violently stretched up to the ceiling. The orange and yellow flames seared the ancient stone without yielding to the strength of the dark force.

He was pulled up onto his toes, but he resisted the compulsion to step forward. The blue-white flames atop the third tier were hypnotic. They too rose into the air, ascending and concealing the statue. A few seconds passed before the flames parted, upon the altar stood a beast made from the blistering flames. The monster was six feet high, six feet wide, and six feet long. The pull of the vortex stabilized, but there was no way they could get the Emerald Tablet to the statue. The beast covered it, owned it. *How can we fix the Emerald Tablet upon the chest of Thoth?* Kevin thought. The fiery beast was blocking the gate to the underworld, preventing the world of darkness from being closed. It pulled back its mouth, snarling, exposing its sharp teeth, daring anyone to move. Fiery wings extended from its back and flapped, fanning the white flames.

Casey moved closer and it growled. Orange flames danced upon its jagged teeth and its scorpion tail slithered back and forth behind it, ready to play. *But nothing is impossible,* Kevin thought. He remembered his bike, his grandmother, the crash, and the day he saw Casey drown. *Nothing is impossible, nothing.*

Rachel was moving forward and started fiddling with Kevin's backpack, feeling for the tablet. He thought she was going to take it out, but she was making sure it was secure. She scrunched her hair into a bun, patted him on the back and walked past him into the open, resisting the pull of the black hole. She turned and looked back at him and said, "It needs a sacrifice and I will be it, for my father. The flames won't hurt if you are of pure heart; you will feel no heat. Remember, mind over matter. Don't give up, we can do this."

Shaun grabbed Rachel by the wrist. "No, I will go!" He stepped in front of her, blocking her way. They stood face to face. Shaun loosened his grip and picked up her other hand, and gently said, "It was my father, he was the cause. I won't lose you again."

Kevin was seeing another person. Shaun was different from the one he had known; he was actually showing concern for another human being. He had been kind to Alex too. Kevin had forgotten Alex was gone; the shocking memory kicked him in the stomach and he doubled over in pain and swallowed back the emotions. As if from underwater, he could just make out Shaun's voice pleading with Rachel not to go. Kevin moved his hands from his knees to his hips and regained control.

"I'll go," Tim said.

"What the hell, has everyone gone mad? This is all a dream, it has to be a dream. I have to wake up. I have too," Kevin said.

Instantly, Kevin felt calm. Sophia had placed her delicate hand on his arm. He could feel her peaceful energy rush through him. "Rachel has to be the one, she has the heart. This is for her soul," Sophia said, still not removing her hand. "We shouldn't take this away from her. Through all her lives she has waited for this moment. Her children and the world will be blessed."

Shaun stormed at Sophia. "Shut up, you're a fucked-up psycho," he screamed. "How can her children, that she doesn't have, be blessed if she's *dead*?" he yelled in Sophia's face.

Sophia, without flinching, said, "She is a gift to her children."

Casey stepped up, trying to calm Shaun and said, "It might seem like a load of crap, but you seriously have to listen to her."

Father McDonald's eyes changed continuously from normal to black pools as he dragged himself towards the flames. Knowing he was witnessing an internal demonic battle, Kevin felt scared and sorry for the priest. Everyone was totally freaking out. Father McDonald had very little strength left; the entity had just about consumed every drop of his light. But he didn't stop fighting. He was trying to speak. Kevin moved closer.

"I must go," he said. "I am the only holy man here. I must be the sacrifice. Stop her."

Kevin had no time to react, because while they argued, Rachel stepped into the flames. She looked calm, as if held in suspended animation, unaffected by the fire or the swirling dark matter.

Shaun stopped yelling at Sophia and turned towards Rachel; she was gone. He ran after her, but the flames drove him back. He couldn't get close enough to reach her. He shielded his face from the flames and screamed Rachel's name. Rachel didn't flinch, or make a sound, just walked on through the orange-yellow flames. She emerged unscathed and climbed up the first twelve steps. Without turning back, she entered the purple-blue flames untouched, and walked up the next set of steps and into the white molten flames. The cave was filled with a sweet smell as if fresh flowers had suddenly bloomed. Kevin moved as close as he dared and saw Rachel exit the blue-white flames. *She is unharmed, not a hair out of place,* Kevin thought. He had expected to see her clothes smoldering at least. She stopped in front of the huge snarling hound, its fiery wings fanning a heatwave, and its tail moved as if it was a separate entity.

It sniffed at her boldness, perhaps intrigued that she dared to enter the flames and stare into its evil eyes. It stepped forward to the edge of the sarcophagus. She didn't flinch. The beast looked behind itself and suddenly two more heads appeared from the rear and faced forward fixing on Rachel. The two heads had been enjoying sniffing its own filth, and were angry at the interruption and the sickening stench of Rachel's unwavering beauty that now filled the cave. The three snouts dripped fiery white mucus. *She looks so small. Why didn't she take the tablet with her?* Kevin thought. *How the hell is she going to get out?* The heads moved inquisitively, seeming to find Rachel of interest and no threat. The beast maintained its stance on top of the statue. The vortex was growing, the cave wall behind the vast ancient steps was collapsing into the black hole. Rachel took another step closer. Saliva the color of coffee dripped from three mouths.

"Do something," Shaun shouted and wrestled with Kevin for the backpack. He took out the Emerald Tablet and ran towards the flames. The intensity of the heat pushed him back again. He tripped forward. Kevin ran to help him, Tim right beside him. The heat of the flames scorched Kevin's face. It was like nothing he had ever experienced. He was worried Shaun was hurt. Tim got to Shaun and started pulling him to safety.

"Get the tablet," Tim yelled.

Kevin snatched up the tablet and turned his back on the flames.

The flames sucked the air from the cave. Kevin had started to feel drowsy, he was slow to think and that's when it happened. A paw surrounded with fire, the size of Rachel's whole body, was extended to her as its claws sprung out and in one swoop sliced the air in front of her. The middle head lifted up and roared. The one on the left bent down and in one motion licked Rachel from her feet to her head. She was covered in brown-black goo that looked like black oil.

We have to do something. Kevin was desperate. We can't just stand here and watch. Shaun and Tim were trying to find another way to get to Rachel. Shaun started to scale the side wall, climbing up and over the flames, but he wasn't going to make it in time.

Just like the day he saw Casey drown, he felt impotent and worthless and didn't understand why God gave him gifts if he couldn't save people from dying. But he had: he had saved Tim, he had saved his dad and Ellen. The hound's wings flapped faster and faster, its paw sliced the air and connected with Rachel. She fell to the ground. Shaun screamed from above, as the beast stomped its paw on her stomach. A second set of claws sprang free and pierced into her abdomen. The monster's massive wings lifted it up and off the sarcophagus. It shoveled Rachel up into its mouth, where she dangled like a puppet with broken strings. Kevin could do nothing but watch in horror.

Shaun pulled himself up onto a ledge, threw rocks at the back of the beast's head screaming, *"Rachel, Rachel."*

A beacon of light, a prism of color, filled the chamber. Rachel was illuminated from the inside out, her entire being glowed. The light travelled from her into the hound's mouth and down into its gut. The beast drew back its snout in disgust and spat her out as if she was diseased. She went flying through the air, over the top of the three sets of flame. The ground cracked open and the orange flames dropped into the belly of the Earth. Rachel hit and bounced off the fallen rocks like a pebble across a still lake. The dirt puffed up around her as she hit the ground for the final time at the bottom of the stairs and slid to a stop. The beast let out a terrifying howl. The heatwave and stench from its mouth was cyclonic, driving everyone back. Kevin sailed backwards and held the Emerald Tablet tight to his chest. He watched as one of its heads desperately snapped blindly at the air. The light went up its snout and surrounded its torso; it roared in agony. Its pain magnified; the heads bubbled and boiled. Rachel's light swamped the hound's entire being, squeezing out the darkness and turning it into falling effervescent lights that fell from the air into the first row of flames. Explosions erupted from deep in the crevasse, rising up into a massive fiery ball and the first row of flames died. The black hole expanded, more of the cave turned to rubble, and fell away into the nothingness. What seemed to Kevin to be an eternity was over in minutes. Rachel lay limp on the dirt, her visible light diminishing; shadows danced on the walls. The vortex was growing and they were all closer to the edge of extinction. The ledge broke from under Shaun.

"Hang on," Kevin yelled.

Shaun struggled to hold on to the rock face; he searched for a foothold and slipped. He fell down to the stone steps and landed on his back.

SOPHIA KISSED Father McDonald on the cheek, despite the demon inside him. "Please don't stop praying. I love you." She felt her hands shaking as she reached into his jacket and pulled his Bible out of his inside pocket, gently placing it in his hands. Mentally and spiritually he was strong. He had continued to fight the physical pain, fighting to stay conscious. She could see the demon swarm to the surface wanting to reach out with Father McDonald's hands and crush her. He wouldn't let it. It was trapped inside him and she could only imagine his pain. "I am so sorry," she said, choking back tears. He was her family; he was the one who cradled her when she wept.

"I won't stop praying. I relish the pain," he said. "This is my gift. We all have a gift. I thought it was to watch over you, but you can look after yourself now. The end of my life is my life's purpose. Look, look at us — all different with different beliefs. Certainty is the glue. I have been a fool." He stopped as his neck swelled. He gritted his teeth in pain, coughed dark blood and moaned. The tension around his throat relaxed. Sophia dropped to her knee to get closer to him to hear him speak.

Panting, he said, "See your spiritual self in all things, Sophia. I'm not going to give up, I'm not done yet. I'll be here for you. End this."

Afraid her voice would tremble she said nothing and untucked her shirt to wipe the blood from his face and kissed him softly again.

Determined, she rose up and shouted, "Kevin."

Kevin had gone to Rachel. He was staring at her, watching her blood quickly spreading, soaking into Terry's sweatshirt, the one Shaun had valiantly given her. Shaun was still on the other side of the deep crevasse, staggering to his feet. He steadied himself, ran down the stairs and on the second-last step, he leapt into the air, swinging his arms and legs and landed inches away from Rachel. Frantically, he tried to stop the bleeding. His hands were covered in her blood; he pressed against her stomach and the blood pooled around his hands. Shaun ripped off his shirt and pressed it down on her stomach to prevent the flow of blood. Tim tore off his hoodie, looped it like a skipping rope and tied it around Rachel's waist. Together they managed to suppress the bleeding; Rachel was very still. Shaun gave a loud, agonized scream.

Kevin stood motionless, hypnotized by the loss of blood and didn't hear Sophia. She felt bad, not wishing to be insensitive, but she knew they had to push on and finish what they started. She spoke a little louder to Kevin, then

Tim suddenly slapped him hard in the face. Kevin snapped out of his trance. Sophia seized Kevin's shoulder and sent waves of energy, calming, balancing his emotions, and said in a controlled voice, "Kevin, we have to do what we came here for, or the pain and suffering will never end."

Tim and Sophia looked intently at Kevin. His eyes were darting left, right, up and down; he was searching his mind for something. Tim slapped him again, this time gently.

"Don't say it, K. I know what you're thinking," Tim said. "Believe in yourself, K, believe in the light. It's in you, man. You've got to trust. I've seen you manifest whatever you put your mind to. It's just like it says on the Emerald Tablet: that which is above is like that which is below. The miracle, I know what it is — manifesting — the ability to create your thoughts and desires in the here and now. You know the saying, be careful of what you wish for because you just might get it. You know this shit, this is in you. It's all up in here," Tim said, tapping his temple. "You think and so be it. Sophia's right. We have to undo what was done. Let's do Jade's entropy thingy and create something new from the madness. No space or time. Now."

"Who are you?" Kevin's eyebrows knotted together and he inhaled.

Sophia untied the sock from around her head and left Kevin with Tim. Kevin had to take responsibility for his abilities and act on his own. She couldn't force him into action. She breathed deeply, and could smell the golden fields at home. She wasted no more time. She ran past the boys, tucked in her locket and like a ballerina, leapt high into the air, gliding over the first crevasse to land on the first step. She continued and ran up the stairs to the second tier. With legs fully extended, her toes pointed forward, she leapt directly into the flames, landing at the foot of the next set of stairs, racing up them towards the white ring of flames. She didn't stop there, or leap over the fire. She ran around it, heading straight for the black hole. Sophia stumbled, fell to her knees. Resisting the pull of the vortex she got to her feet. Balancing on the edge of darkness she looked into the silky black whirlpool. It was silent. Rocks and stones floated in the slipstreams, spiraling anticlockwise, disappearing into its evil eye, into oblivion. Sophia closed her eyes. Her hair violently lashed her cheeks. She ignored the desire to look down, the urge to fall into the vortex. *Focus, damn it!* Her aura, a rainbow of colors, glittered; she channeled all the energy deep into the Earth, anchoring her to the edge. Slightly wavering, she reached into her shirt for her locket and held it in her palms. She squeezed it in her hand like she had done a million times. This time, the Penelope's web face disengaged from the rest of the amulet and sat in the palm of her hand. Sophia stretched her arms above her head, and magenta liquid energy poured from the center of the amulet. Twelve channels of curved magenta light emanated from the stars of Solomon like lasers weaving a web, a barricade that held the swirling vortex at bay. Everything behind her went quiet as if they were in the eye of a storm. Sophia looked over her shoulder and could see Casey, Jade, Kevin and Tim. Shaun was pressing down on Rachel's abdomen. She couldn't see if Father McDonald had continued to struggle or was dead. She prayed he was alive. The second blue ring of fire extinguished. Casey and Kevin looked as if they had prepared themselves to jump before the blue flames had died; motionless they gazed down into the crevasse's infinite space.

UPON THE LAST TIER, the flickering white flames momentarily allowed Jade to catch a glimpse of the statue's full beauty. "Look at that! It's amazing," Jade shouted.

"She is, isn't she," Casey replied.

"No. Yes. Not Sophia, the statue. It reminds me of an Egyptian anthropoid coffin," Jade said, shaking her head in amazement. "They were made of gold and inlaid with semi-precious stones." Jade stepped backwards, away from the others, giving her room to jump. "What are you two waiting for? Jump!" she yelled at Kevin and Casey.

Jade sprinted past them and jumped, mimicking Sophia's action without the grace. Arms flailing, she fought her way through the atmosphere, searching for leverage, for that extra inch. Jade started to descend. *Oh shit, my angle of velocity is all wrong.* She came close, but not close enough; her toes skimmed the lip of the fissure and it gave way. She dug her fingers into the dirt, sliding, searching for purchase. Jade screamed. The sound of the billowing horn above had penetrated the depths of the cave as if it had been in the chamber with them.

Kevin yelled at the top of his lungs. "Hang on, Jade, we're coming."

Jade's fingers had latched onto two protruding stones, her feet frantically searching for anything to take the weight off her arms. She dangled like a rock climber and felt the moisture in the palm of her hands. *They're not going to make it, and I'm not worth them dying for.* Jade saw Kevin and Casey clear the edge. Together, they hung over the side and wrapped their strong hands around her wrists and pulled her up to safety.

~

Sophia held her position. The amulet was doing all the work; the laser light web was arching over the abyss like security sensors. It was wavering slightly and she wasn't sure how long it would hold. They had to hurry. Sophia slowly moved, bent down and placed the amulet between her feet. It shook and vibrated on the spot and started to spin on one of the points. She pushed it back down onto the edge of the pit and it held its ground. She walked backwards, away from the black whirlpool with its swirling demons of death. Sophia turned towards the others and headed to the last barrier of flames behind the four cubed columns, the last ring of fire that surrounded the sleeping statue.

Sophia ran up the twelve steps to where Jade was trying to decipher the symbols on the columns between the dancing flames. Out of breath, she said, "We have to go into it. We have to step into the fire, Jade. You can see the symbols better on the other side. We have to keep moving. I don't know how much time we have left."

"We can't just step into the flames," Jade said. "That is just not logical. I can see no evidence suggesting we have to walk into a blue-white flame which is, like, at least nine thousand and ten degrees." Kevin took Jade's hand and Casey took the other.

"You're serious. We are really going to do this. Oh, God."

Sophia took Casey's hand and said to Jade, "Now you're getting it. Certainty, we can do this. Let go and it will be okay. Close your eyes."

Jade closed her eyes and saw Great Turtle beckoning her forward. Jade let go and together they stepped into the flames.

11

JEWELS OF GOD

The absent heat of the blue-white flames returned as soon as they stepped upon the final tier. Casey quickly pulled everyone away from the roasting temperature at their backs. They struggled against a magnetic force emanating from the golden statue of Thoth that was preventing them from moving forward. Casey felt the force was curved, circular to the touch. He ran along the outside looking for a way to get closer, but he could not go beyond the surrounding four columns.

"Look over here." Jade waved her arms in the air. "The cavity on the chest, it's the second and third part of the message, Sophia. That statue is the golden rock representing the guardian of the underworld and the empty cavity is at its heart. That must be where the Emerald Tablet belongs. We have to somehow get over there.

These columns must have something to do with the force field. They are common symbols: earth, wind, fire and water," Jade said. "Give me your water, K," and she poured it over the pillar that had the sign for water carved into it. Nothing happened.

"The number twelve has come up a lot," Kevin said. "The maze —"

"The stairs," said Casey.

"So how can these four columns relate to the number twelve? Besides the obvious divisions," Kevin said.

"The twelve signs of the zodiac," Sophia said.

"Who's a Scorpio?" Jade asked.

"Me," Casey said.

"Is anyone Taurus?"

"I am," Kevin replied.

"You're an Aries?" Jade said, raising her eyebrows at Sophia.

Sophia shrugged her shoulders. "I might be. I was born on the twenty fourth of March. Would that make me an Aries?"

"You have to be. I am an Aquarius," Jade said.

"Find the column with the element that represents your star sign: Taurus earth, Aquarius wind, Scorpio water, and Aires fire. Go."

Casey stopped at the column at the bottom of the statue's carving of squiggled lines that represented water. Sophia was opposite at the head, Kevin was on the east side, and Jade took up her place on the west aspect of the statue.

Kevin grabbed a handful of dirt from the cave floor. Casey was ready with the last drops of his water.

"I don't have a flame," Sophia yelled as she tried to get close to the white flames to steal a little of its fire.

"Wait, I think I have a box of matches in my backpack," Kevin said. He rummaged around before pulling out a box of redheads. Grinning, he ran over to Sophia, then back to his pillar and grabbed another handful of dirt.

Sophia took out a match, and left another one sticking

halfway out. She placed the box on top of the column ready to light up the whole pack at once.

"Ready?" Jade yelled. "Everyone on my count: one, two, three, now!"

Casey slowly poured the water over the top of the column, watching Sophia strike her match and drop it in the box, which ignited straight away. The columns began to moan, slowly descending into the ground and a large stone in the wall was slowly pushed out. Water gushed from its opening into the crevasse. The final ring of fire behind them was extinguished by the rising water, but the magnetic force did not wane.

They still couldn't get any closer to the statue. It continued to repel them.

"Damn it," Casey said. Jade watched him as he shuffled his feet, changed his stance, stuck his neck out slightly and lowered his head. He concentrated on Kevin's backpack.

"I can feel that!" Kevin said. "My stomach is doing a backflip."

Casey guided the breastplate out of the haversack and into the air, levitating it above Kevin's head. He stabilized the tablet and slowly walked as close as he could to the statue. *If we can't go around or through the force field, maybe Casey can go over it*, she thought. He raised it up, up, high in the air and gently brought it down to hover over the chest of Thoth.

"We're in! Go, Casey." Jade stood at his side cheering him on as he flipped it in the air, searching for the right angle, trying to place it like a piece of a jigsaw puzzle. It wasn't locking onto the golden statue.

"What is the rest of the message?" Jade asked.

"No end and no beginning —" Kevin said.

"To face the heavens and the emerald light will glow, the light will be returned," Jade said.

SHAUN COULD NOT STOP the flood of emotions flowing any more than a pebble could hold back the gallons of water flowing in the surrounding crevasse, Rachel thought, feeling Shaun's despair radiating into the cave around them. Tim stood by Shaun's side, helpless, unable to help as she slipped in and out of consciousness. Rachel felt sorry for them both: Shaun having to witness her death, and Tim the reluctant spectator to Shaun's torment. Rachel opened her eyes and tried to speak. *Oh, God, that hurts.* "You have to ..." she said. Blood trickled from the side of her mouth and she tried to wipe it away. She drew two short quick breaths and had a fit of coughing, spraying blood. Her lungs were filling up.

"Oh, dear God, take me, not her," Shaun said, cradling her head. "Please not now, please, I just found her. Oh God, no, please."

Rachel's vision was fractured as she looked up, following Shaun's gaze, and saw the others passing through the flames and moving towards Thoth.

Shaun looked back at her. She stared into his beautiful eyes. His strong arms held her against his chest. To die in his arms is enough. It would be so easy to just close my eyes and let go. He had come back for me, he had found me.

"Casey ..." she said.

The horn above cried out again to the heavens, silencing her words. The beast had pierced her lung and abdomen, the pain not to be endured. She could feel the warmth of the pooling blood as she shivered with the cold, aware her life was slipping away. She was glad she had sacrificed her life to destroy the beast, having fulfilled her purpose. *No regrets,* she thought. She tilted her head back, reached for Shaun's face and he moved closer to her lips. She could smell his sweet breath. "Casey ..." she whispered again. "Tell Casey to flip it. Writing down, circles up, face to heaven." Her breathing labored; she waited, still couldn't catch a breath. She was drowning and couldn't stop it. "The Emerald Tablet ... once it is on the statue ... only you can activate it, Shaun, only you."

"Shh, quiet, save your strength," Shaun pleaded with her.

"You must ... before the final blowing, before the last sound of the horn ... lay the stones in first formation: mercy, strength, harmony and ..." Before Rachel could finish, she folded within herself and crossed the threshold of her inner door out into the vastness of the universe, free of her body, free of pain.

SHAUN FELT the stones digging into his thigh as he drew in a jagged emotional breath, then thought, *Could these be the stones?* Rachel filled his senses; she touched his soul and made him know what love was. Her eyes glazed over and closed. "Rachel, no, Rachel, no, you can't die. I won't let you die." He laid her flat on the ground and started compressions.

Shaun wiped the sweat and tears from his eyes on his shoulder. He stopped and quickly fished the leather pouch from his pocket and tossed the stones to Tim, and said, "I'm sorry. I'm so sorry for what I did to you. Give those to Casey and tell him what she said." He breathed for Rachel and pressed down on her chest again resuming the compressions.

"She said only you can," Tim said.

Shaun ignored him, focusing on counting, breathing for Rachel, trying to keep her heart alive. He felt a sudden emptiness and his soul screamed; he believed he would explode into a billion pieces. "Rachel, come back, please God, don't take her from me. I promise to love her for all eternity. Please God, not Rachel, please!"

Shaun was blinded to everything around him and he no longer cared for the world; everything he wanted was slipping through his fingers. He didn't want to live if Rachel died. Tired, he stopped, pulled her to him and cradled her body. He rocked back and forth, then laid her down, recommencing the compressions and yelled at Tim, "GO!"

Tim picked up the pouch and jumped over the crevasses, raced up the steps onto the platform and handed Casey the stones.

"You're going to need these."

Sophia took the stones and Jade crowed with excitement and said, "Oh my God, can this get any more complicated? Wow! They are Platonic solids. They have different elements. This one, for instance, represents fire, and has six edges and four faces so it's a tetrahedron. This one represents earth and is a hexahedron having twelve edges and six faces."

Tim took it out of her hand. "It's a cube!"

Jade dismissed him and continued twirling a twelve-edged gemstone that looked like two pyramids joined together and said, "This one is an octahedron; its element is air." Her finger tingled as she touched the tip of the next one that was blue and its shape resembled a pointy transparent soccer ball. "This one is, I think, an icosahedron, element water, and it has thirty edges and twenty faces. It reminds me of what Rachel said about the one of the circles on the tablet. Chesed, mercy, which is blue and represents air, has the same properties as this solid. Maybe that's where this gem belongs, in that circle; maybe the stones are formed to connect all the elements. By laying each stone in the right circle, the energy will flow along the pathways."

"Slow down," Casey said, trying to secure the tablet. "That's a lot of maybes. I haven't even got the tablet in place yet and you want me to position the stones."

Sophia touched the emerald gemstone. "And what's this one?"

"The dodecahedron, the universe, and that one is a tetrahedron. This one is my favorite," she said. "It looks like two stars merged into one. It is named merkaba and this one is Metatron's cube, which has the element of earth."

Tim immediately picked up the transparent cubed stone and Jade could see inside it were thirteen suspended spheres. Twelve small crystallized rods came from the centers of the twelve spheres into the middle sphere, connecting them all. "Check this out. It's like the drawing on the Emerald Tablet and on Sophia's medallion," she said.

Tim, pointing at the dodecahedron, said, "It reminds me of a flower and — what do you call it? One of those superfood fruits ... a pomegranate. What about the three marbles, Jade?"

Jade dismissed Tim's reference to marbles. "This is what Shaun had in his pouch; they were so much more than gemstones." She examined the remaining gems. "All spheres. A sphere contains all forms and all measurement is equal." The sphere took her breath away. "This is beautiful." She felt connected to them and couldn't quite find the right words to express how they made her feel. She held it up to look into its content: she beheld a tiny universe floating inside it. Quickly she studied the other two and saw wisps of colored clouds, like gases, continuously moving, folding, fusing together; creating sparks of light. "Continual potential. It's like the birth of a star," Jade said. "This is incredible. This is absolutely mind-blowing. These are phenomenal and they are the key to the lock." She looked over at Shaun. He sat on his heels by Rachel. *We did have the keys all along*, she realized.

"What about this last one?" Kevin picked up the clear quartz sphere and stared into its depths. He dropped it back into Sophia's hands, as if it had given him a shock. "Wow!"

"What?" Jade picked it up and turned it around and around. "What did you see?"

"My ... me ... looking back at myself ... as if I was inside the crystal, looking out."

"What does it all mean?" Tim said.

Jade's eyes moved from right to left and up and down, thinking, constructing ideas and thoughts before she spoke. "$S = K \log W$. Entropy, a measure of disorder," she mumbled. "Life is filled with entropy. This whole situation reeks of disorder, it's totally dysfunctional." She held up the sphere with the spiraling gasses. "These gemstones will help us to close the gate to go back to the seed level perhaps. Back to the past maybe. I'm not sure, but certainly back to a state where we can create a new future within this reality, the element of earth. It's a paradox. Life is a paradox."

Tim took in a deep breath, loudly exhaled and said, "She's lost it."

CASEY BLOCKED out the chatter around him and the images of the ever-expanding silent vortex. The others seemed to be forgetting about their purpose. It was as if all the logical thinking was actually the darkness stalling for time. Casey focused on the Emerald Tablet and following Rachel's instructions. He jerked his head as if he was shaking the hair off his face and immediately the breastplate flipped over with the circles facing the dark roof of the cave. It floated down, feather-slow, as Casey placed it on the statue.

It locked into place.

"K, look at that," Tim said, hitting Kevin in the arm. Everyone's attention zapped to Casey. They held their breaths, expecting an explosion of light, something miraculous, anything to swallow the darkness and consume the power of the vortex. Nothing happened.

Nothing at all.

12

LIGHT OF THE ENDLESSNESS

He's doing it, Sophia thought. The stones vibrated and moved in their hands, lifting off from their palms.

"Now to lay the stones." Casey held them suspended with his mind. They spun in the air three feet above the statue. The markings on the Emerald Tablet cast a faint glow. Casey's intensity increased. Like an orchestra conductor his hands moved in all directions and the stones darted in the air under his command. Sophia felt the pulse of the repelling force around the statue. It was unyielding. The black hole expanded, stretching the force field. The amulet was shaking violently, losing control. She had to do something, but what?

"There must be a way," Casey said. "Which circle and which stone. It was created by the light of God. How are we going to come up with the correct formation? We need more time."

"We have to go back to the seed level, return to the beginning," Jade said.

"Back to where? Where's the starting point? Where do we start, Jade?" he said anxiously.

"Earth, we have to start with the Platonic solid that represents earth, the hexahedron, the cube, and ascend to ..."

There is only one seed level I know and that's the oneness of the universe. Sophia sat down and closed her eyes, ignoring Jade, and opened up her mind to the heavens: she stepped through her internal door into the endlessness of the universe, no limitations, all desires waiting to be realized. She could have floated forever; it was like soaking in a luke-warm bath. She wanted to stay. *I must find the solution of the stones.* She accelerated along her timeline, searching for the telling moment in the future, forgetting to anchor herself to the present.

Sophia levitated off the ground and the gems gravitated towards her, gliding through the air away from the statue and tablet to hover around her.

"Sophia, what are doing? Sophia," Casey yelled as he lost control of the stones.

Sophia felt her aura swelling — the essence of each color changing from warm reds and oranges to cool blues and violets as it continued unfolding — and she recognized her soul expanding, ready to receive the abundant wisdom of the universe. Her aura turned to a shimmering magenta light, a beacon to the darkness. She felt her sense of self melting away; her connection with physical reality was disappearing as she searched along her timeline. Like an untethered cosmonaut, she floated in space, waiting in the silence of the universe. She was in love and wished to stay.

Cloaked by inner peace, her sense of self drifted away.

~

Casey headed for Sophia's floating body, she was almost transparent, like a ghost. "Sophia!"

Father McDonald's body contorted in pain, fighting against the demons inside him for control. He yelled, "Don't touch her!"

Kevin could do nothing to stop Casey. He reached out and touched Sophia's dangling foot and was thrown into the air like he had touched an electric fence. Casey sailed backwards, passing Shaun, Rachel and Tim as he tumbled down the set of stairs and over the edge into the second-tier crevasse. Kevin sprinted after him, and could see Father McDonald crawling on all fours, bent out of shape like a dog. *He's going to maul him*, Kevin thought, and that's when Father McDonald stretched his arm out to Casey.

"Ahhhhhhh," Father McDonald screamed as Casey let go of the edge and latched onto his arm pulling it out of its socket.

Kevin didn't want to begin to imagine the pain Father McDonald was in. He could have sworn he heard tendons and bones snapping. Casey was frozen, glaring into Father McDonald's black eyes.

"Climb," Kevin yelled, looking down at them from the top of the stairs.

Casey used Father McDonald's arm like a rope and quickly climbed up and over his body. "Thank you," Casey said and ran to Sophia. She had floated higher and soon she would be out of his reach.

Casey ran faster than Kevin had seen anyone run before — up the stairs two, three steps at a time, to the third tier and hurdled over the crevasse. *He looks like he's flying*, Kevin thought. He glimpsed Father McDonald on all fours tip over the edge, as if in slow motion, and without a sound, disappear into the crevasse.

"Sophia," Casey yelled. "Sophia. Come back, Sophia."

Sophia was flickering.

She reminded Kevin of a light bulb about to explode. Casey reached for her foot again. Kevin knew Casey would be electrified and maybe even injure Sophia. He fixed his eyes at the ground, imagining millions of tiny particles of golden light weaving a rubber mat under Casey's feet before he touched Sophia. *The mat will ground Casey's energy*, he thought, *soaking it up like a sponge and sending it into the belly of the Earth.* Casey touched Sophia's foot and, as he did, her amulet, on the edge of the vortex, lost its hold. It was flung into the air and skipped like a pebble, hitting Casey on the side of the face, slicing open an old scar. Suddenly it was like being in the middle of a storm.

THE MAGENTA FORCE FIELD DISAPPEARED. The repelling magnetic energy of the statue receded. Sophia's aura started to turn inward, creating an up-draught, repelling against the darkness. She was imploding.

The sound of the two forces is like being caught between two massive jet turbine blades, Kevin thought.

SOPHIA LOOKED out at the expansion of the universe, and watched a dot on the horizon moving closer and closer, growing into myriad shapes and colors. Something was forming: a blur, an image, a memory. It's Shaun. This wasn't the future, this was the past: he was a child playing on his bedroom floor with the gemstones, making different patterns. Then it changed, and Shaun was no longer a child but a troubled young man who was out of control, devastated by the loss of his mother and Rachel. Then the images changed again to the present day. His shoulders were slumped, tears rolled down his face, his grief splashing over Rachel's lifeless body as he willed her to live.

Shaun knows the combination! she yelled inside her head. She turned and looked right, then turned again and looked left. Her excitement vanished. The endlessness of the universe was magnified and that's when she noticed she had forgotten her lifeline — she was a lonely astronaut floating in the silence of space. She squashed the panic, allowing the peace to spread within. Free of chaos, her surroundings took over. Her aura continued to expand, brighter and more colorful than any nebula in the galaxy. Sophia was merging back into the endlessness from which she came when from a far, far away corner of the universe Sophia thought she heard a whisper. There it was. She started to feel again, to remember her physical being, the sensation of being inside her body. She listened, moving her thoughts towards the sound. She searched her mind and again heard a whisper. She knew this sound and saw a flash of an image, then suddenly she felt heaviness, as if rising from an ocean pool.

"Come back, Sophia, come back." Casey held fast to Sophia's foot, screaming over the noise of the two repelling forces. "Sophia, come back, we need you, come back."

A flash burst into her solace as her consciousness fully awoke. She screamed inside her head, *Casey, I hear you. I'm lost. Is Kevin still with you? Kevin, are you there? Can you hear me?*

$$\sim$$

Yes, I hear you. How are you doing that? Sweat dripped from Kevin's temples. It had taken intense concentration to manifest something as simple as an industrial rubber mat, and it barely held together, the atoms jumping as if they would pull apart at any moment. Casey and Sophia had an enormous amount of energy pulsing between them.

"Show me the way back."

Casey held onto her ankle determined not to let her disappear. Kevin could see his fingers through her leg.

"Let go, Casey, you need to move back," Kevin said.

"No, I'm not moving. I'm not leaving her like this, she needs to be grounded."

"We don't have time! You have to let go or we will all die. Trust me, I've got her," he said, tapping himself on the temple.

Casey looked up at Sophia. Then he let go.

Kevin concentrated on creating a pathway to Sophia and the image of the mat evaporated. He sat on the ground, his pulse racing. He was so nervous he wanted to scream, or run. He clenched and unclenched his jaw, breathing in through his nostrils and out of his mouth. He shook out his arms and rubbed his hands on his knees, and tried to relax. Involuntarily, he inched across the cave floor, pulled by the expanding swirling black hole. He ignored the external mayhem as Sophia had and went inside himself. He stood before the old door he kept locked. The feeling of the ground beneath him disappeared as he too began to rise. Kevin could only imagine the look on Casey's face.

All his life he had avoided the door, but now he touched the tough hardwood. It was inviting, warm. He reached up and felt the cold metal of the first bolt and slid it back. He imagined he wiped his sweaty palms on his pants, and reached out for the second latch and pulled it back quickly. He lingered, braced himself and took hold of the third bolt and pulled it all the way back. The door unlocked, opened, and he was looking out into the expansion of the universe. Kevin stepped over his sacred threshold into nothing and everything, imagining a carpet of glittering golden light unrolling towards the essence of what he thought was Sophia. He stepped upon the carpet and ran towards her.

A REMOTE MEMORY of lemon soda came into her mind. Sophia felt something. Searching her expanded mind she knew someone was coming. Her nose was tingling, as if she had one, and it smelt a sweet smell: *a memory of soda pop*. No, it was sweet-smelling and it tingled in her nose like effervescent bubbles. *Nose — I have a nose again*, she thought, and then she tasted the essences of life popping on her tongue like pop rocks. The connection grew stronger. Ahead, a conveyor belt of sparking golden light appeared. She moved her mind towards it, finding Kevin. An awareness of someone else was also behind her, and she felt goosebumps along her arms and wanted to shiver. Kevin was nearly in sight. The sensation behind her grew. She turned, dreading what was there. Sophia decided to move to Kevin.

"Sophia, wait!" It was Rachel. "I have seen the concealed light. It is greater than any light you have ever seen or felt. It will be as bright as the birth of the universe, and you will all be incinerated. Only the purest of souls, the greatest of sages, can merit this sight. You are all key to the survival of the world, and Kevin is the final key."

"Yes, he's coming. That's him, Rachel, come with us."

"No, you don't understand."

"Yes, I do. Come with me. Please."

"My fate is in Tim's hands. Tell Shaun he must do it. Go

now. Seal the gate, Sophia. There are only two more sets of blowing. Can you still hear them?"

Sophia listened. "No." She looked again, back at Kevin. He wasn't getting any closer, he seemed to be running on the spot.

Rachel said, "He can't come any closer. If he does, he won't be able to return to his body. He will die, and you will die, everyone will die. You have to meet him halfway.

"Go! Go now, Sophia!" Rachel screamed.

The urgency became overwhelmingly real and Sophia felt like she was in a nightmare, climbing stairs that turned to quicksand. She willed herself to run, imagining one complete step after another. She visualized her legs moving, seeing her knees lifting up, higher and higher as she ran. She saw the image in her mind of running in shallow water, until she was flying towards Kevin as if zooming above the water. Then suddenly she found herself skimming the surface of the golden pathway Kevin had created.

Sophia began to feel the millions of atoms that formed her body being drawn from across the universe, aiming for the spiritual essence of Kevin. Sophia yelled out to him, "It's Shaun! He knows the combination of the stones." She flew above the golden carpet Kevin had unfolded in the astral plane for her.

"Hurry, Sophia, we have to get back. My body is going to combust," Kevin said, just as the impact of Sophia's spiritual essences sent his physical body into convulsions. He could feel his nose dripping with blood.

SHAUN AND TIM took turns and did what they could to keep the blood circulating through Rachel's body. It was Shaun's turn. He knew they all thought it was pointless, but he didn't care. *I won't stop.* Tim was a big help and didn't ask questions.

He could see the others on the altar. Casey was trans-fixed, watching Sophia's body flare. It sparkled and flick-ered, infused with light, and solidified. Her energy was drawing into herself, causing the gemstones orbiting in her aura to start falling away. Kevin's body trembled. Casey tried to reach out for him when simultaneously everything was tumbling down: Sophia, Kevin and the stones. Jade scram-bled to catch the gems, throwing herself towards the swirling dark matter with her arms outstretched as if she was an outfielder catching a fly ball. She missed one and it rushed towards the vortex. Kevin's limp body hit the ground hard on top of the stone. Casey, the true knight in shining armor, was there to break Sophia's fall. Dazed, Sophia and Casey clumsily got to their feet and pulled away from the vortex.

"Shaun!" *Is she calling me? Why would she be calling out to me?* He had been doing compressions for so long his body was acting purely on muscle memory now. Sophia, as if she carried a heavy burden, tucked her head down and quickly descended the flights of stairs, yelling his name. "Shaun! It's you. Only you know the sequence."

What now? he thought, seeing them all coming his way, except for Kevin, who stood by the altar watching, holding his head. Sophia's silky hair was flying everywhere as she jumped down the last few steps and rushed to his side. Out of breath, she said, "I saw Rachel. Shaun, she said you are the only one who knows the sequence of the Platonic stones."

He looked down at his bloody hands. "I don't know any combination," he yelled, resuming the compressions.

Sophia put her hand on his shoulder. It was soft and delicate, cool on his hot, bare skin.

"She's gone, Shaun."

He shook off her hand. "No, I won't give up. In the past ten years she never gave up on me." Tears dripped off his chin.

"It's okay," Tim said. "I'll do it. I promise I won't stop till you say. It was my turn anyway. Do it, Shaun." Tim knelt on the opposite side and slowly, as if unrolling dough, slid his hands onto Rachel's chest. The tips of his fingers gently nudged Shaun's away.

Jade's face was flushed. She was more than a little freaked out. "Shaun, move, damn it!"

Shaun couldn't move. A soft blanket was draped around him. He had an image of Rachel as he remembered her, but she had turned into the woman who lay beside him now. He saw, as if looking through a keyhole, everything moving away from him. Jade pulled back her hand and slapped him in the face. *Whack!* Rachel's image was gone, replaced with a burning sensation on his cheek.

"You fake," Jade screamed. "You don't care about her. If you cared, you would fight her fight. She guided you here for a reason, she needed your help. So what the fuck are you waiting for? Get up and put those stones in order and finish this."

Something snapped and Shaun's face burned, his fists clenched. He wanted to punch her. "You bitch." He stood as Tim kept up the compressions. "A swift kick in the face would shut you up and send you back to wherever you came from. How dare you, who the fuck do you think you are?" The desire to hit her was compelling, growing, boiling up inside him. He should beat her like he had wanted to beat his drunken father for letting his mother die and killing

Rachel. *Rachel, he didn't kill Rachel. She was here. I killed her. I couldn't keep her safe.* The shadows of doubt were prowling around Shaun's head. *I'm just like my father. He couldn't keep the one he loved from dying and I couldn't keep Rachel from dying.* For the first time in Shaun's life he felt sorrow for his dad. He now understood. It must have been hell for him to live without her. The guilt his father must have felt. Shaun looked at Tim. He looked exhausted, pumping away on Rachel's lifeless body. "Let her go," Shaun said. His voice was shaky and barely audible. He cleared his throat and said a little louder, "Let her go, she's not there. You can stop." He got down on his knees and kissed her cheek and whispered in her ear. "I love you. I'll finish this. I will see you in my dreams."

Tim looked up and said, "Not yet. You go. I know what I'm doing."

Jade flung her arms across her face, ready to block his blows as he reached out for her. He pulled her arms down and pulled her close to him. Her nostrils flared, he could feel her breath; his own tasted sour. His cheeks were salty, sticky with sweat and tears as he hugged Jade and said into her ear, "Thank you."

Shaun hadn't even noticed Kevin until his friend vomited. It splashed on his runners and was sucked weirdly backwards by the growing vortex. Soon they weren't going to be able to resist its pull. The guy looked like he was going to drop.

Jade helped Kevin down and propped him up against the step. She grabbed his face and stared into his eyes, checked his ears and head. "You look concussed."

The vortex had stretched above the statue and was building momentum. It was the biggest, darkest cloud

Shaun had ever seen. This was going to be the mother of all storms.

"Shaun, let's do it," Sophia said, climbing the steps, and she jumped. No — she flew from the pull of the vortex up onto the third tier and tumbled and somersaulted to a stop at the base of the golden statue.

At the top of the last tier he could see the devastation. The second half of the cave was disappearing into nothingness. He concentrated on the stones, not knowing what to do with them. Sophia was in his peripheral vision. "Please, hurry," she said. Her hair and clothes were flapping all over the place. It was incredible that her small frame hadn't been sucked into the darkness like everything else. Sophia urged him on gently. She was always gentle. *Rachel was fiery and forceful, absolutely amazing, fun, beautiful, full of life*. He wished he had jumped from the Jeep that night and stayed with her. He hadn't known she survived. He had been nothing but a little kid. Shaun glanced into Sophia's soulful eyes and her eyes very slightly squinted, and at that moment they both knew, as if cymbals had clashed, that things were about to change forever.

Sophia called, "Jade! Jade! Jade, tell Kevin. Tell Kevin to get ready, we need a way out."

"What?" Jade yelled back, running halfway up the stairs.

Shaun, seeking protection, sat with his back against the dazzling statue, thinking that it was really just a coffin. All its magnetic propulsion had changed into a tiny hum. Casey and Sophia gathered around him as if Shaun was the last burning flame. They huddled over him, guarding the stones and him from the vortex. Shaun tossed the stones on the ground between his legs. He didn't know what to do. He had never given any thought to patterns and formations. He picked them up again, closed his hands around them, and tossed the gems, watching them tumble and roll on the dirt like he was some high roller in a casino. But he wasn't, he was just some punk kid with a shitty life. The image of playing a game with Alex came into his mind.

Shaun scooped up the gems and got to his feet, stretching to his full height, completely exposed to the vortex, allowing the energy to drag him across the floor. *What is the world going to be like without Rachel, anyway? Maybe this is humanity's destiny and who am I to get in the way?* He felt light as a feather as he glided across, to the edge, closer to the point of no return. The sound was deafening, his mind went silent, and that's when he saw Jade leaning over the statue, touching the tablet now set in its chest, and saw her bracelet and the Emerald Tablet come to life. A radiance of white-blue light came from the bracelet, the markings lifting from it, spiraling into a 3D hologram, entwining together as the hologram traveled around the tablet. Alex appeared in Shaun's silent mind. He watched as Alex showed him the last game he had taught him at Casey's house in England and Shaun saw the order in which he had laid them before he began. *That must be the pattern ... well, it's a pattern,* he thought. All of a sudden, a wave of clarity rushed over him and he felt hope. Rachel lived to correct the mistake his father had made. She wanted to heal the world. He had to destroy the vile creatures that escaped that day; he had to eliminate the dark angels and close the doorway.

Shaun realized he had foolishly allowed himself to be dragged nearly to the edge of the swirling black hole. Spellbound, he saw Rachel's dark, long curls in the outer rim of the whirlpool, like leaves down a drain, swirling and swirling. Shaun was sinking.

Maybe none of this is real; maybe I have a brain tumor, just like Mom, and I'm delusional. For a second, he nearly believed it was Rachel. He felt like he was in a rip. His mom had suffered. She had taught him to swim before he could walk, and surf as soon as he could stand. Always warning him about the undertow and rips. Your board goes where your eyes go, she had said. He started to panic, his eyes glued to the slipstream of evil. He pulled back, away from the darkness. *Not now, oh, please God, not now. I know what to do. I can do this, I know my purpose.* He fought to gain control of his mind and body: he pulled and inched away, shuffling like a crab back towards Sophia and Casey. His chest, back and arms felt like his skin was being ripped off as if it were a shirt and his jeans were giving him the biggest wedgie ever.

Casey held onto the statue, while Sophia, Jade and Kevin made a human chain. Kevin held out his hand. Shaun took hold. They made a human shield around him, protecting him. Quickly, he ran his hand over the cold breastplate of Thoth and began laying the stones. There was no force field now. The 3D hologram of glittering letters swirled and danced and twisted above the statue, blocking the negative vacuum.

I hear you little buddy. One more game, Alex. Shaun got to work on placing the stones. Starting in the bottom circle of the middle column — the suspended thirteen circles that looked like a reflection of all that was below it — he placed the first stone, Metatron's cube. Moving up to the next circle, he placed the octahedron and he kept moving up, placing the merkaba in the circle Rachel had called harmony. Swiftly, he positioned the remaining stones on the outer columns, leaving the top three in the shape of a triangle till last. He was moving back and forth, right to left, up and down, checking the order. Shaun stopped as if he had all the time in the world, reviewing his handiwork. He focused intently on the last three spheres, not quite sure which one went where. The noise around him intensified. *Think, damn it.* The sphere that Jade said reminded her of swirling gases — the formation of stars —definitely belonged at the top right, he decided, and the other at top left. He held it tight, rubbing it like an Aladdin's lamp between his hands. He held it up to his mouth and kissed it like he had done as a kid and placed it at the pinnacle of the Emerald Tablet's design. Shaun looked over his shoulder to where Rachel lay. Tim had kept his word. They weren't the only souls he could see. An angel, twelve feet high, stood over Casey, Sophia, Kevin and Jade.

The walls of the cave disappeared and were replaced with the blackness that was moving in on them. The noise was so great his own thoughts sounded like they were a long way away. Shaun looked at the Emerald Tablet; still it had not come to life. Kevin, Casey, Sophia and Jade stared at him with anticipation as the stones locked into place, but again nothing happened. Shaun reached down into his pocket and pulled out the last of his memories of the first day he met Rachel: a black onyx stone, and placed it face down between the top three spheres. The Emerald Tablet of Thoth radiated blinding light, while, above, the last bellowing horn cut unnervingly through the dense energy. A brilliant shaft of light was cast down from the sky, towards the Emerald Tablet.

The circles and gemstones turned to liquid light that flowed along each pathway, crisscrossing between the circles in a predetermined formation. Sophia pulled the group back as the light joined forces with the Earth circle and Metatron's cube, the hexahedron. All the gemstones were oscillating, and the light was returning, rising up the pathways to the pinnacle.

"We have to go!" Sophia screamed. No one moved. They stood united, rooted to the spot. She yanked on Casey's and Jade's hands and leant towards Kevin, shouting, "You're up, Kevin!"

"What!"

"She said you're on, K."

"You have to get us out of here." Sophia glanced in the direction she last saw Father McDonald and began to cry. His life was her life, she couldn't remember being without him. She closed her eyes and felt his spirit all around her, and she turned. He was with her. He would always be with her. The lock and key, the emerald-green tablet, had been returned to Thoth. *Go, Sophia,* she heard him say in her mind. *Go now!*

HIS FIVE FRIENDS looked like warriors. He imagined Kevin couldn't concentrate with the high piercing scream. The light and the darkness was clashing, making it impossible to focus. Tim smiled, Jade reached out and took Kevin's hand and yelled something, and that's when Tim saw the vibrant colors, the rippling wall that had come to life under Kevin's persuasion. There wasn't too much of a harmonious hum, or the sound of the tear in the universe as the doorway opened. There was only the battle, the vortex losing control.

Jade and Sophia stepped forward into Kevin's gleaming curtain of light and were absorbed into the gentle flowing wall, free from the darkness.

Casey corralled Shaun. He must have been afraid he might run back to die with Rachel. But before they entered, Shaun turned back to Tim. It was too late to say or do anything as Casey pushed him into the soothing wall. Tim remembered how it had cooled his sunburn and healed his broken leg.

"Come on," Kevin yelled.

Reluctantly, he stopped the compressions. "I'm right behind you." He jumped up, ran. The black hole was imploding and the ceiling vanished. The column of light passed through the third center circle and grew so bright it was becoming hard to keep his eyes open.

"It's just us," Kevin yelled to Tim. "You go and I will close it behind us."

They both went to jump, but Tim stopped. He could see Shaun on his knees behind the sea of animated color. Sophia put her hand on Shaun's shoulder as if to console him. Tim turned back for Rachel; he wasn't going to leave her. He hadn't performed CPR for the last twenty minutes for nothing. *Focus, Tim, it could still work. His original idea could still work. There is no reason why not.*

Tim sprinted to where Rachel lay. He quickly dragged her into a sitting position, put his head under her arm, and lifted her over his shoulder. He had underestimated her weight and staggered slightly. He was close to the wall and could see Kevin about to step back through. The light ascended to the Emerald Tablet's second last circle. Tim no longer felt Rachel's weight, or felt his own limbs for that matter. The light penetrated and vaporized every dark corner of the chamber, pushing him into the air as flashes of brilliant light exploded in a fireworks display that moved across his eyelids. But just before he closed his eyes, he had seen the horrors of the underworld trying to escape from the vortex, screeching and howling in pain in the all-consuming light.

Tim closed his eyes tight, imagined his legs were still there, and walked blindly with Rachel over his shoulder, in what he hoped was the direction of the world Jade called Athanasia, the parallel world.

A SONIC BOOM pulsated through the membrane as the cave exploded. Sophia, sheltered from the blast, couldn't help reacting and covered her eyes. The wall sparkled and bowed, arching under the force, creating a cocoon protecting them. Light, color and sound rippled and flashed like a cosmic storm. The cave disappeared. Tim and Rachel were propelled by the blast through the closing doorway. The darkness consumed everything, the evil falling into oblivion as the vortex of dark matter collapsed in on itself and a final atomic explosion erupted: the birth of a star.

Sophia sent a thought message to everyone to turn away from the wall, to walk into the luscious forest before them, and not to look back. Above them, outside the membrane, a darkened sky filled with streaks of silver and golden sparks of light like a magnificent meteor shower. The dark angels fell from the sky consumed by the light. They watched in awe.

Sophia sent out another guiding message, gently urging them on. We need to move forward into the future. Don't look back. There is no existence beyond this moment. We have to step into the future.

They all knew what each other was thinking. There wasn't a thought amongst them that was hidden; there was no space between them. Kevin wanted to turn back for Tim. Shaun wanted to run back for Rachel, but he believed this time she was truly gone and he was glad that she wasn't alone. Tim had been with her to the end. Sophia longed for Father McDonald's comforting prayer. There were other thoughts, some of which Kevin had imagined sounded like Tim and Rachel. Shaun heard them, too, and he couldn't contain himself any longer. He started to cry, wanting so very badly to turn around.

Don't turn, he heard Sophia think.

Had they made it through? Shaun wondered. How could they have survived the blast?

Tim was mesmerized by Rachel's fluttering eyelids. Her beautiful, emerald- green eyes were opening and looking up at him. She was confused and dazed.

Tim helped her to her feet. Kevin had so much belief that he heard Tim's thoughts, he wanted to turn back and see if what he was hearing was real. Rachel went to look over his shoulder. Tim grabbed her face to stop her. He had heard Sophia tell them not to look back and quickly covered Rachel's eyes. Her lashes tickled his palm. He remembered how he felt after seeing his leg broken one minute and healed the next. He wondered what Rachel might be feeling. He walked on.

Kevin could hear them both inside his mind. Rachel felt very strange and confused as she too had heard Sophia's words inside her head. Facing into the forest she opened her eyes and saw Sophia, Casey, Kevin and Jade, plus her handsome knight in shining armor, Shaun. Rachel hugged Tim and the sides of their faces were lit by the exploding light as she whispered in his ear, "I never doubted you for a minute." She let go of his hand and drew the air into her lungs. She felt so fresh and alive and started walking towards Shaun.

Shaun had stepped forward with a heavy heart into the future. He could feel Rachel was still with him, her spirit strong, when suddenly he thought he felt her touch, a soft hand interlocking with his. He knew it was Rachel, but how could it be? He didn't want to look to his side in case it wasn't her. He rubbed where the bullet in his back had been. Tim had continued CPR right up till the last minute, but how — ? Then he heard Tim's thought: *I don't remember you telling me to stop, so I brought her with me.*

This must be what a mental breakdown is like, Shaun thought. It was all too much. The hand squeezing his was soft. He had to look, he had to. It was Rachel.

"You and Tim kept my heart pumping," she said, not realizing all she needed to do was think it and they all would know what she wanted to say. "You kept my body alive and my soul reclaimed it. Shaun, you told me the first day we met, you would come back for me. Not once did I doubt you."

13

BECOME THE CREATOR

The seven friends walked through the majestic rainforest. Kevin had tried to open a doorway home, again and again, but it just wasn't happening.

"Let's just sit for a while," Sophia said.

Kevin sat amongst the fluorescent green leaves watching the tiny blue insects.

Each time they stopped, he would look beyond the surrounding membrane, and his eyes would feast upon the universe as if they were a part of it, as if they were floating amongst the Milky Way.

"What do you think is happening out there?" Jade asked.

They all sat around and seriously gave it thought. It was like listening to multiple radio frequencies and Kevin was learning to dull out the others' voices in order to hear his own thoughts. "Maybe there are still some rescue teams helping people somewhere. People have to pick themselves up. They have to pull themselves together and get through this."

"Come on," Sophia said. "Let's keep moving."

Jade quickened her pace to catch up with Kevin and Sophia. "You know, when everything gets back to normal, or close to it, you can travel anywhere in the world, K. Can you imagine the enormity of your skill in the world? I wouldn't mind paying a visit to the Big Apple."

"I don't think we should tell anyone about Athanasia. We need to protect it." Kevin saw images from Jade's mind of New York and she was biting into a big slice of pizza. Kevin imagined what New York might be like now. Jade's colorful image dissolved. Kevin remembered that awful day, so long ago. So much sadness, fear and anger and he had been unable to understand or process the emotions he felt from the adults and the world around him. It made his heart ache even now, thinking about the pain and suffering. Suddenly, before he finished the thought, they came upon an outer wall and beyond the membrane was a dusty grey New York street, as he had just imagined. The sky above the street curved like the dome of a snow globe and sparkles of light danced upon a long velvet sash of time unrolling from the heavens. The street was the center of Kevin's giant snow dome. Energy was falling from the heavens to the street, scintillating, coming together as one compound; a building formed, glowing with color. It was Jade's pizza restaurant. The rest of the street remained grey and congested with fallen bricks and mortar, nothing but rubble. There wasn't a bird in sight. There were lifeless bodies; so many, the debris beneath them could barely be seen. Kevin started moving away from the horrific scene. How long had it been? Time had little meaning for them in Athanasia and this was the first time they had seen the outer world. Glittering light floated down from the heavens settling as gently as snowflakes upon the bodies. "If only one person would move, just one." Kevin said. "We have to go help them."

"Wait," Casey said reaching out for Kevin holding him back. "Something is about to happen."

They all stopped, waiting, watching as time continued to unfold in front of them and beyond. Holding his breath, Kevin paused. *Just one person. Come on, one person.* They shared the thought, willing it to happen. A brick moved, an arm moved amongst the rubble. An ashen face lifted and looked out at the vastness of destruction around them. The seven ran forward to the wall to cross over and help, but for the first time the wall was impenetrable. They looked on. It was a woman. She stood and looked into the sky before she reached down to the person next to her, pulling them up. Then another person stood and helped the person next to them. A chain reaction was occurring among the people the sparks of golden light had touched. They were rising; color was returning to the world one hue at a time. Not everyone rose. Only a third of the fallen had stirred; the others remained lifeless, lost to the darkness forever. The people who had risen tried selflessly to help those unmoving. They dropped back to their knees and cried for the strangers who were gone.

Tim put his arm around Kevin. "Let's go home, K."

KEVIN EFFORTLESSLY OPENED a doorway back to his family, back to Casey's bedroom where he had sent his dad and Ellen only hours ago. It seemed like forever.

It was morbidly quiet back in Casey's room. No one spoke. The sunshine was streaming through a hole in the roof, highlighting the broken wooden beams littering the polished floor. Worried that Daniel and Ellen lay pinned beneath, Jade and Kevin quickly leapt into action, climbing over the beams like it was some wacky obstacle course searching for them. Without asking, the others helped lift the planks of wood when, abruptly, everything floated up to the ceiling. Casey smiled with his arms raised in the air like the conductor of an orchestra.

Casey saw Daniel's ashen face, his lips dry and cracked like a riverbed in the outback. Ellen started to stir.

"Mom!" Jade said, and slowly helped her to a sitting position.

"Dad," Kevin said.

He looked afraid to touch his dad. *Maybe he wasn't breathing*, Casey thought. Then dirt puffed around his nostrils slightly.

"Dad," Kevin said again. Daniel's eyes moved behind the lids and his eyebrows rose as if trying to pull the eyelids open.

Tim spat on the edge of his shirt and wiped Daniel's lashes clean before Daniel tried opening his eyes again.

Casey was standing next to them with his arms raised to the ceiling. "Guys, my arms are getting a little tired," Casey said, slowly backing out of the room.

"Dad, can you stand?"

His dad's voice was harsh and raspy, nearly unrecognizable. "Kevin. Ellen?"

"I think she's okay. Can you stand?" Kevin asked again.

"Water."

Tim ducked into the bathroom and came back with two soaking wet face cloths. He gave one to Ellen and one to Daniel. "Suck the water out of the cloth and let's get you out of here."

Ellen was grateful and sucked deeply.

Daniel did the same, then wiped his face and put the cloth around his neck. He held onto his left leg and lifted it out straight and cringed. "It's okay. Oh, my throat. Everything is stiff," his dad said, massaging his calf muscles. "It's been at least a few days. As soon as we came through the … the … portal, the ceiling collapsed. We yelled and yelled but no one came. I'm worried about the rest of them. I haven't heard any sounds, K. Where's Father McDonald?"

"He didn't make it."

His dad searched his eyes for answers.

Kevin and Tim each put their shoulders under Daniel's armpits and helped him to his feet.

The wood hovered in the air. Daniel ogled it. "Marvelous, absolutely marvelous," he said to Casey.

Jade and Shaun aided Ellen into the hallway. "How long has it been?" Ellen asked.

Jade answered for Kevin. "Actually, it probably hasn't even been twenty-four hours for us. Let's get you out of here before Casey's arms drop."

"What?" Ellen said. "It's been at least two days, maybe three."

"Casey?" Sophia said. "You don't have to raise your arms. You know that, don't you? It's your mind that controls the wood."

They went from room to room and still hadn't found anyone in the house. In the kitchen, Casey said, "This whole place has been cleaned."

"It looks pretty messed up to me," Kevin said, looking around.

"No, I mean there are no lost souls. Not a flicker of residual energy. Everything feels new somehow." Outside, a dog barked. Casey opened the back door and Lucy jumped all over him.

"Hey girl." The dog pulled away and ran down the basement stairs.

The basement door was missing from its frame. "Wait," Daniel said, but it was too late. Casey was on the dog's tail.

One by one they stepped over the door that was lying in a wonky position at the bottom of the stairs. Lucy had stopped at the entrance of the tunnel and looked back and waited. Casey took the lead. He cautiously made his way to the place they had stashed their supplies, passing where he had found the young girl's bone. *Come on, Amy, make a noise, anything.* He stopped and touched the limestone walls searching for Amy and Terry.

"This way," Casey said, rushing down the next tunnel. "I can feel them, down this way."

He raced through the tunnel afraid of what he might find. Scared, Casey moved carefully, as if not to disturb the dead. He stepped into the opening. The air felt fresh. It should have been musty; it puzzled him, because it actually smelt fresh and vibrant. The tunnel opened up ahead and in his mind he saw the red-bearded man, Amy's great- great-something-grandfather, was looking over his shoulder at them before he disappeared leaving them with the silence.

Shortly, they found the group huddled together lying on the ground as if asleep: Amy, Terry, Callie, Kath and Sally. Somewhere amongst them were Joe and Molly, and the Book of Splendor, which was twinkling.

Daniel rushed past him and felt the nearest body for a pulse.

Casey felt the presence of life and expelled a breath when he realized he had been holding it. *But are they all alive?* They lay as lifeless as rag dolls.

Shaun and Kevin moved to Callie, stepping into the radiance of the fluttering lights from the book. Casey knelt by Amy, scared to touch her. Ellen came and knelt beside him and checked her pulse and pupils and smiled.

"She's alive, Casey. She's alive."

Sophia found Joe, the red string still tied to his wrist, his arms outstretched around Sally and Kath, protecting them. "Joe is alive too," she said excitedly.

Casey held onto Terry and Amy's hands, watching Rachel reach for the edge of a pink blanket sticking out from under Callie's arm. It was Molly. Rachel tightened the tiny blanket around Molly and picked her up, holding her close. Rachel softly spoke and rocked Molly in her arms and kissed the crown of her head. Molly's sudden scream shattered their fears. There was no room for silence as she continued to cry. Callie stirred, searching for her crying baby. Amy and Terry began coughing, and reached for each other. The dog licked Kath on the face, until she pushed it away. Sophia wedged herself behind Kath to reach Joe.

"Sophia," Casey said. "Is he okay?" He knew Sophia had only known Joe for a short time, but had grown very fond of him, and having lost Father McDonald, Casey was afraid she had lost Joe too.

Lovingly, Sophia put her hands on Joe's big face. "Hey you," she said as Joe blinked and smiled at her. She hugged him tight and cried.

"Whoa, hen, why the tears? I knew you'd be back. Where's the Father?" He looked around and painfully pushed himself into a sitting position. Sophia sat down and lifted his arm up over her head and nestled into him. Joe squeezed her shoulder. "When was the last time you ate? You're wafer thin."

"He sacrificed himself for us." Tears filled her eyes. "Are you hurt?"

"Not hurt, just very stiff, lass. We've been here perhaps a few weeks. There was an awful crash and that's the last I remember."

Casey closed the book of light and smiled. Terry and Amy were locked in a hug. They opened up their embrace for him to join them.

"This is incredible," Ellen said. A smile burst through her tears of joy and she tasted the salt that lingered on the edge of her lips. "Callie, my dear friend Callie."

Callie looked towards the voice, perhaps waiting for her eyes to adjust, not believing her ears. She leant heavily against Daniel and gradually stood. She didn't bother brushing the dirt off her face or reining in her joy and relief. "Ellen, is that really you?"

Ellen held her arms out and walked forward. They stood in a tearful embrace. Jade twirled her bracelet on her wrist. *It now looks like any other bracelet,* Casey thought, watching Kevin move closer to Jade, smiling. Casey looked from one person to another; everyone was shaken, but would be okay. Rachel handed Molly to Daniel and without hesitation, kissed Shaun, before tightly embracing him.

Callie had pulled back and wiped her tears. "I have your specimens." And nodded her head to the little blue esky half buried in the dirt.

"What's in the esky?" Casey asked.

"My life's work," Ellen said. "The reason I was kidnapped. The cure for cancer, the vaccine. You name it, I think I can cure it," Ellen said.

*** The End ***

ACKNOWLEDGMENT

I would like to thank my high school English teacher and my supportive family and friends for their encouragements. Thank you, to the invaluable editors, Linda Funnell and Stephanie Smith who have been a tremendous support. No book is complete without the vital service of editors, proofreaders and great book cover designers. Finally, I would like to acknowledge the professional project management services of Joel Naoum from Critical Mass, who made it possible to share my story with you.

Enjoy this book? You can make a big difference

Reviews are the most powerful tools in my arsenal when it comes getting attention for my books. Much as I'd like to, I don't have the financial muscle of a New York publisher. I can't take out full page ads in the newspaper or put posters on the subway.

(Not yet, anyway).

But I do have something much more powerful and effective than that, and it's something that those publishers would kill to get their hands on.

A committed and loyal bunch of readers.

Honest reviews of my books help bring them to the attention of other readers.

If you've enjoyed this book I would be very grateful if you could spend just five minutes leaving a review (it can be as short as you like) on the your favorite online bookstore, which you can access through my website as well as book two and three in the series.

https://jmhartwriter.com/buy-now/

Thank you very much.

GLOSSARY

Al-mawet – Mawet means death, al-mawet is no death. The spelling varies within different religious text, but they all have the same meaning.

Arrow of time – the direction of events; movement in time is generally forward.

Athanasia – means timelessness, everlasting life. Athanasia is referred to as the parallel world/dimension.

Dark matter – a negative energy force. In this story the dark matter also contains micro shapeshifting demons.

Dovesti zhenshchinu – pronunciation for Russian довести женщину. English translation: bring the woman.

Dunny – toilet.

Fair dinkum – an expression in Australian slang proclaiming a truth about a statement.

Intel – slang for intelligent person. As in geek. (Created by the author)

Merkaba – two tetrahedrons combined. Mystically it is a channel for the descending energy of the universe and the ascending energy of Earth. Spiritual tool of transformation.

Metatron's Cube – a geometric shape/solid. It has thirteen equal circles. Lines from the center of each circle extend out to the centers of the other 12 circles.

Outback – A remote area of the country.

Platonic Solids – shapes with equal sides. The five platonic solids are; tetrahedron hexahedron, octahedron, dodecahedron and icosahedron.

$S=k \log W$ – the second law of thermodynamics. Entropy – a mathematical formula that represents the lack of order or predictability. A slow decline into disorder or randomness. (Our characters want to reverse this state of being or create a new one from the disorder the negative thoughts of man and the micro beasts have created.)

Sphere – a round solid with equal distance from its center.

Stickybeak – an overly inquisitive person.

Talking stick – a ceremonial stick that is passed around a group of people giving the holder the right to speak.

The devil's puppets – the people controlled by the micro demons. Those infected by the virus which is the dark matter.

The Tree of Life – a spiritual concept that has been used and referred to throughout the centuries in mythology, religion and philosophy to name but a few. It refers to the interconnection of life and its evolution.

Vremaya dlya distsipliny – Russian pronunciation for Время для дисциплины. English translation: time for discipline (a good whipping in this story).

If you enjoyed the first book in the Emerald Tablet Series, please go to www.jmhartwriter.com for the next book.

ABOUT JM HART

Now semi-retired, JM moved to a peaceful county town
south of Sydney, to focus on her grandchildren and writing.
JM Hart is the author of The Emerald Tablet Series, and
The Chronicles of the Supernatural. She makes her online
home at http://jmhartwriter.com
You can also connect with JM Hart (Jeanette) on:
Facebook, Instagram, Pinterest and twitter.
And you should send her an email at
author@jmhartwriter.com if the mood strikes you.

www.ingramcontent.com/pod-product-compliance
Lightning Source LLC
Chambersburg PA
CBHW030648110726
47901CB00002B/611